To Skye & Siena

love from Nicky 30 Aug 2003
xx .

This book belongs to:

....

....

MY BOOK OF

Mystery

STORIES

MY BOOK OF

Mystery

STORIES

Written by
NICOLA BAXTER

Illustrated by
ANDREW WARRINGTON

This is a Parragon Book
First published in 2000

Parragon
Queen Street House
4 Queen Street
Bath BA1 1HE, UK

ISBN 0-75253-671-0

Produced for Parragon by
Nicola Baxter
PO Box 215
Framingham Earl
Norwich NR14 7UR

Designed by Amanda Hawkes

Additional illustrations by
Richard Duszczak

Printed in Italy

Contents

The Mysterious Mask

When Jake was a very small boy, he used to think that his granny's house was just like the one in the story of Little Red Riding Hood. It was deep in a forest and, although there was an overgrown lane ending at the gateway to the garden, there were also lots of little paths leading to it through the trees.

The first time that Jake didn't want to go to Granny's house, his mother was puzzled and not very sympathetic.

"Come on, Jake! Time to get in the car!" she called, snapping her briefcase shut and struggling into her jacket.

"No. Not going," mumbled Jake, playing with his trains on the floor.

Mrs. Clarkson looked at the clock.

"Mummy hasn't got much time, Jake. Be a good boy, now. You know that Granny is going to take care of you today. You'll have a nice time. You always do. Maybe she'll let you help with her baking again. Chocolate-chip cookies! Mmmm!"

But Jake hung his head and said, "No! Not going."

His mother sighed and pushed her hair out of her eyes.

"I'm not arguing, Jake. You can bring your trains if you like. But hurry up now! Don't be difficult."

But Jake, seeing her advancing on him with a determined look, scrambled to his feet and ran behind the sofa, from which, he knew by experience, it was very difficult to extract him.

Several tense moments later, Jake was being carried, screaming, to the car, and Mrs. Clarkson was very nearly in tears herself. Only when she had strapped Jake firmly into his seat, retrieved her briefcase and bag, locked the house and clambered into the driving seat did she feel calmer and look in the mirror at the red-faced little boy in the back.

"You can have your music on," she said. "Now stop crying. I don't know what the matter is. You love Granny, don't you?"

"Yes," said Jake, "but what about the wooluffs?"

"The wooluffs?"

In the end, Jake's music didn't go on. The journey was spent in his mother gradually finding out that Jake was very frightened of the wolves that prowled around Granny's cottage. Of course, there weren't any wolves at all and, at first, Mrs. Clarkson couldn't imagine where he had got the idea from. When he mentioned Little Red Riding Hood, she understood at once and laughed.

"Yes, Granny's house is a bit like the one in your storybook," she said. "But I promise you, there are no wolves nearby at all. You're quite safe there."

Jake was finally persuaded that he didn't have anything to worry about. Still, for nearly a year after that he used to lead his Granny round the house when he first arrived, checking in all the cupboards and under the beds and in the dark place under the stairs that there were no wolves at all lurking there. Jake's mum explained what it was all about, and Granny was very understanding. She even made a big sign for Jake to hang on the front door. It said: Wolves, Keep Out!

Mrs. Clarkson had to work long hours and her job sometimes meant that she had to go away for a couple of days. Jake always went to his Granny's at those times. He had his own little room, with some of his toys and books always kept in it and a selection of his favourite videos down in the living room.

But best of all, Jake loved to play in the garden. The house that he lived in with his mum was in the city and didn't have a garden, so creeping through the shrubbery, climbing the apple trees and digging about in the little plot that Granny had prepared for him was wonderful. While he was still small, he never went into the woods beyond unless he was with Granny.

"It isn't that there is anything frightening there," Granny was quick to reassure him. "It's just that it's very, very easy to get lost."

Jake didn't want to get lost. He was still quite a nervous little boy. He was happy to play in his own imagined world in the garden, although as he got older, he did become more and more interested in peering over the fence to see if he could glimpse anything exciting through the trees beyond.

One day, in the middle of summer, Jake's mother had to go away for three whole days. Jake was at school now, but the summer holidays had started. Of course, he went to stay with Granny.

"The strawberries are ripe, Jake," she said, "so we can pick those tomorrow. And I'd like you to help me pull nets over the raspberries. If not, the birds will eat them all before we have a chance."

But that night, as Jake lay in his cosy bed beneath the eaves, a huge summer storm thundered over the little cottage.

The rain rattled against the window and lightning flashed through the sky. Granny came in with her dressing gown on to see if Jake was all right.

"I don't know when I can remember such a bad storm at this time of year," she said. "I'm afraid the fruit will be ruined. I don't imagine many of the apples will still be on the trees after this. Just listen to that wind! You're not frightened, are you?"

"Of course not! I'm eight!" Jake protested. "There isn't anything to be worried about. You're not frightened, are you, Granny?"

Granny laughed.

"No, I'm not. And I'm glad to see you're such a big boy now. Try to get some sleep. We'll have to go out and look at the damage in the morning."

But in the morning, the rain was still pouring down. Granny sighed as she made the breakfast.

"I'm not sure my old roof can stand this," she said. "I'll have to go up later and take a look. We may need some buckets to catch the drips."

"Go up on the roof?" Jake tried to imagine his granny clambering up ladders in the storm and failed.

"No, go up in the attic," she replied. "Neither of us is going out in this."

The morning wore on as Granny tidied up and rang a few of her friends to see how they were getting on in the wild weather. Jake was bored. He looked at several of his books and watched some sport on television. Then, in the middle of a game, the lights went out.

"I thought this might happen," said Granny, peering at him. The cottage was gloomy inside, even though it was still morning. She hurried off to find torches and candles while Jake unplugged the TV.

The rain had eased a little during the morning, but now it lashed down with new force. Granny looked anxious.

"I'm going to have to go up into the attic," she said. "Do you want to come, too, Jake?"

She could see that he looked bored, and she couldn't even offer his favourite cookie-making to pass the time.

There was a trapdoor into the attic and a ladder that could be pulled down. Granny went first, holding a torch, and Jake followed her. There was only just room for them to stand up in the middle of the attic. The roof sloped down all around. Luckily, there were no drips.

"What is all this old stuff?" asked Jake, staring at the boxes and trunks that were packed beneath the beams.

"Most of it is rubbish," said Granny, "that I haven't found time to throw away. You can have a look through it, if you like. I'll leave you the torch."

Jake was more than happy. He'd seen TV programmes where people found treasures in the attic that made their owners rich. He perched the torch on a nearby box and lifted the lid of the nearest trunk. This was a job that might take all day. But who knew what he might find?

It was well into the afternoon when Jake found the mask. He was shining the torch into the depths of the fourth trunk when he suddenly gasped. Two shiny eyes were staring back at him. At the bottom of the trunk there was what looked like the head of a wolf, snarling and revealing its yellow teeth. Looking closer, he saw that it wasn't a real wolf's head. It was carved out of wood, and when he lifted it from the trunk it proved to be just a face. It was a mask. Jake forgot all about treasure. He carried the mask down to Granny and asked where it had come from.

"I haven't the faintest idea," said Granny. "I don't believe I ever saw it before in my life. It's probably something that came from my uncle's old place. There are trunks of his that I've never even opened. He went a bit odd, you know. Then he disappeared."

"It's a wonderful mask," said Jake. "It's so real-looking. I had to look really closely before I could tell it was wood."

"If you ask me, it's a bit sinister," said Granny. "I don't care for the look of those fangs. Do you remember when you were tiny? You didn't like the idea of wolves at all, then."

"That was ages ago," said Jake. "I was only little. I'm not stupid like that now. Do you think I could wear this?"

"The ties at the back have rotted away, but I could make some new ones," she replied. "But lunch first!"

It was a late lunch by candlelight, but soon after they had finished, a shaft of sunlight streamed through the window and the rain stopped. Granny flung open the door.

"It's over," she said. "Look, blue sky! You can go outside now. Jake?"

But Jake didn't need telling twice. He was already past her and running down the garden, ignoring calls about boots and coats.

Under the apple trees, Jake paused. It was difficult tying the new strings at the back of the mask by himself but he did it in the end. For the first time, he peered out through the glass-covered eyes.

Suddenly, the garden seemed very different. It wasn't a place of fun and games any more. It was full of scents and sounds he had never noticed before. Somehow, he knew that there was a rabbit under the hedge. There was a bird's nest in the bushes. And now, something new... Jake crouched quickly, his breath coming hard and quick. Danger!

It was Granny, shaking the table cloth out of the back door, but Jake didn't feel anything but fear. Turning, he ran on silent feet away from the house, his heart thudding. The wet leaves soaked his clothes as he ran past, keeping low, alert for every movement in the bushes, every sound from the branches.

The fence! What had always seemed so familiar suddenly filled him with fear. There was no way out! He was trapped. Jake ran desperately along the fence, his eyes keenly searching for a gap. Instead, he came to the gate.

Jake had never tried to open the gate. It wasn't locked but the latch looked stiff and difficult. Now, it was the only thing on his mind. He tried desperately, pushing at the metal, but his hands were stiff and he couldn't move his fingers. He scrabbled at the wood with his nails, and little growling sounds came from his throat. It was hopeless. Desperately, he ran on. There it was! The gap he'd been looking for! In the storm, a branch had fallen and pushed over a section of fence. In a second, Jake had bounded through. Relief rushed through his body as he ran off into the trees.

It was drier in the forest. The thick leaves above had protected the forest floor from the worst of the rain. The cool, clean scent of washed leaves filled Jake's nostrils. As he loped along, birds fluttered up into the branches and tiny animals scuttled into their homes. Jake threw back his head and sniffed the aromatic air. He had never felt happier.

Meanwhile, back at the cottage, his granny came out to look at the damage done to the garden by the storm. She called to her grandson as she walked around and was surprised when he didn't answer. Then she found the broken fence. She, too, was suddenly afraid.

Far away, among the trees, Jake heard her calling. He stood motionless for a moment. Then turned his back and slowly slunk away. The voice meant nothing to him.

All the afternoon, Jake prowled through the trees. He was looking for something, but he didn't quite know what. A wolf is a pack animal. Although Jake didn't realize it, all his senses were directed at one thing. He was searching for his own kind—a kind that was definitely no longer human.

But all those years ago, what his mother and grandmother told him had been correct. There were no wolves in the forest. They had been hunted and killed hundreds of years earlier. It was the descendants of those hunters that walked silently through the forest today, looking for sport.

The gunshot cracked through the forest like a whip. Jake stopped in his tracks and felt a sick fear sweep through him. For a moment, he was dazed. Where had it come from? Then the scent of the hunters came to him, faint on the breeze. And something worse. Dogs! A fraction of a second after he recognized their scent, he heard the frenzied barking that meant that they, too, had sensed an alien presence in the forest. The sound seemed to swell in his ears, deafening him. For a moment, he couldn't move, then, with the salty taste of terror in his mouth, he turned and fled, running like the wind through the trees.

Afterwards, Jake never forgot what it was like to run for his life. For years he could hear the drumming of his heart in his ears, his rasping breath as he pushed himself to run faster and faster, the feel of the forest floor beneath his feet.

Suddenly, ahead of him, he saw the broken fence. It didn't look like safety. It looked like a trap. Snarling, he turned to fight, tossing his head defiantly.

And at that moment one of the mask's new strings broke. The wooden face fell from him. He was no longer an animal facing its foe. He was a frightened boy, his chest heaving and his mouth dry. Tears ran down his cheeks as he turned and stumbled towards the house—the safe house where a wolf had never been seen.

Jake never wore the mask again, He threw it into a corner of the attic and tried to forget.

Twenty-five years later, Jake's own children went often to visit their own granny, who now lived in the house she had inherited from her mother. One day when they returned, Molly had a carrier-bag clutched in her arms.

"It's just something Grandma gave me," she said. "It's a secret."

Jake didn't think anything of it, until he heard the howling…

Mark's Marbles

When Mark Mack lost his marbles the jokes at school went on for weeks. You can imagine the kind of thing...

"Lost his marbles? I thought he lost them years ago."

"Lost his marbles? I didn't know he had any."

Strangely enough, Mark wasn't at all worried about this. He was so worried about what had actually happened that he had no worrying left in him. He tried to explain to his friends about what he had seen, but they simply laughed. He was so worried, he even tried to explain to his father, who was a scientist. Now, if you had ever met Mark's father, you would know that things would have to be desperate indeed before you turned to him for help. He simply didn't live in the same world as the rest of us. He was the kind of person who didn't know what a cornflake was but understood everything about a tiny planet billions of light years away. He could barely tie his own shoe-laces, and, as Mark had feared, he was completely useless when it came to explaining missing marbles.

"What do you mean they vanished right in front of you? That's simply not scientifically possible. If you've got a couple of hours, I'll explain why…"

Mark tried to escape, but when his father started talking about atoms, photons, the speed of light and quantum theory, it was like a prison sentence. The two hours stretched to four and for the last of those Mark was actually asleep. When his father noticed this at last, he relented.

"If you're interested," he exclaimed, "we can go into it further tomorrow." It was strange that Professor Mack, so keen on examining the evidence in his own work, never thought to consider what falling asleep might mean in his audience.

The next morning, Mark rushed out to school as quickly as he could, pretending not to hear his father's, "Ah, Mark, as I was saying…" as he passed him in the hall. But once pedalling along the cycle path, Mark had time once again to think about his marbles. Yes, I know it sounds funny, but here's what happened…

The day before, Mark had eaten his lunch in the cafeteria as usual with his good friends Jumbo and Frizz. While Jumbo was quite unlike his nickname, being the skinniest boy in the school, Frizz had a shock of blonde hair that stood up all around his head. All the boys in Mark's class had been asked to bring along something for a history lesson. It had to be from a family member and show an aspect of life in the early part of the twentieth century.

Frizz, whose great-grandmother had been on the stage, brought along an old poster for a variety show from the 1920s. It was for the Apollo Theatre and promised such delights as "Nerina, the Nightingale of Egypt", "Powerful Pete Presley, Strongman", "Andrei Analytov's Angels" (the dancing troupe in which Frizz's great-grandmother performed) and "Billy Budger—you'll die laughing!"

"Do they have nightingales in Egypt?" asked Jumbo, who was of a strictly practical turn of mind.

"I've no idea," said Frizz. "Can you really die laughing?"

"Well," Jumbo pondered. "I suppose you could die and happen to be laughing at the time, just as you could happen to be eating a hamburger or having a bath. Do you think many people die in the bath? Would you mind having a bath in a tub that someone had died in? In fact, if you moved into a new house, how would you know if someone had died in the bath or not? Or anywhere else, for that matter."

"Stop! How did we get on to this subject? Please don't let's talk about people dying in the bath," said Frizz. "It'll put me off ever getting in one again."

"You don't anyway, do you?" said Mark, holding his nose.

There was a short interval during which Frizz tried to shove baked beans down Mark's collar and Jumbo tried to clean escaped beans from Frizz's poster. When the attentions of Mr. Keppler the headmaster meant that order was restored, Jumbo showed Frizz and Mark what he had brought. It was a long stick with wooden spikes on the end.

"It's called a dolly," said Jumbo. "You used it for washing."

"It's a bit big for cleaning your ears out with," said Frizz. "And don't say, 'How would you know?' Mark!"

"It's not for washing people. It's for washing clothes," explained Jumbo. "You put it in the water and swished it around. They used them before they had washing machines. My great-aunt Avis gave it to me. She said it was her mother's."

"Did it work?" asked Mark, looking doubtful. "I thought they took clothes to streams and hit them with rocks."

"That was in the Middle Ages!" Frizz protested. He had a better grip on history than the other two because his mother was a history teacher in another school. "I should think this dolly thing worked pretty well. Machines only swish clothes about, after all. What did you bring, Mark?"

Mark showed them the marbles that his grandfather had given him a couple of weeks earlier. The gleamed red, yellow, blue and green in the light.

"He used to play with these when he was a boy," he said.

"Looks a bit limited to me," Jumbo commented. "There can't be much you can do with them."

"Apparently there are all sorts of games," said Mark. "I wrote down some names. Here: Skelly, Dobblers, Puggy, Poison Pot..."

Frizz and Jumbo rolled about laughing.

"Anyone for Dobblers?" asked Frizz in a posh voice.

"Well, I think they look good," said Mark. "Look, some of them are really unusual. It makes you wonder how they made them."

But Frizz and Jumbo were still giggling, so Mark put the marbles back in their bag and carried them into school.

After stopping at his locker to pick up his history books, Mark went straight to class. He could have sworn afterwards that he didn't put the bag of marbles down once. It was too big to put in his pocket, so he swung it by the drawstring at the top as he walked along. Once, he thwacked a radiator in passing and the clang that rang out made him worry that he'd broken some of the little spheres of glass. As soon as he reached his place in the history classroom, he undid the string and carefully emptied the marbles out on to the desk.

That was when they disappeared. One minute he was looking at them. The next minute, they were not there at all. Mark rubbed his eyes and looked again. The desk was empty except for the bag the marbles had been in. He looked under the desk and even in the desk. The marbles were nowhere to be seen.

Five minutes later, when Frizz, Jumbo and the rest of the class came in, they found Mark crawling on the floor.

"I hate to ask," said Jumbo, "but what exactly are you doing?"

"I've lost my marbles!" wailed Mark, which sent the rest of the class and Mr. Staple the teacher into hysterics.

As I said, the jokes about Mark's missing marbles ran and ran. But long after the most annoying first-former had forgotten to point and giggle whenever Mark went past, Mark himself was still worrying. He *knew* that he had seen the colourful glass marbles rolling across the desk. He *knew* they had disappeared a second later. He also knew that no one in the world was going to believe him.

As the time grew nearer for another visit from his grandfather, Mark became even more anxious. What if the old man asked to see the marbles? Over the days that followed, Mark thought of possible things to say. He was a boy with a methodical mind, so he wrote them down. In the end, he had a hundred and two.

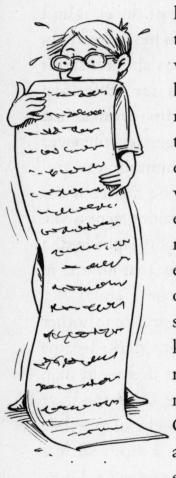

The reasons on the list ranged from, "I left them at school", which was at least reasonable but might result in a request to go and find them, to "They were eaten by next-door's dog", which didn't sound likely even to Mark but at least meant they were gone for ever. Or did it? Mark's overworked imagination saw his aged grandfather kidnapping the dog and rushing it to the vet for marble-removal treatment. Or, worse, following it around with a hopeful expression and a poop-scoop. Ugh!

By the time Mark's father went to meet his dad at the railway station, Mark was in a dreadful state. During the evening meal, while his grandfather asked about school, football and the size of Mark's feet (he was growing quite fast at the time), the boy shuffled and went alternately pink and pale. He dreaded a question about you-know-what.

But the marbles were not mentioned. Mark went to bed with relief—and didn't sleep a wink all night. It's bad enough to lie awake worrying about spots or exams. Being sleepless about marbles is worse because you feel stupid as well. By the morning, Mark was so worked up that when his grandfather looked up from the breakfast table and said, "Good morning, son. How are you today?" the words that came out of the boy's mouth were, "Oh, marblous. Thanks. Oh…"

Mark's father had already gone off to his laboratory. Mark's grandfather gave his grandson a long, hard look and asked the inevitable question.

"Ah, yes, that reminds me. How did you get on with those marbles? Were they okay for your history class?"

Mark gulped and not one of his one hundred and two answers came into his head. The only thing he could think of saying was the truth.

"I lost them," he mumbled. "One minute they were there and the next they were gone. I'm sorry."

But the old man didn't look at all concerned.

"Oh," he said, "I expect they came home. I didn't think to look. I'll give you a call when I get back. No need to worry."

"But... But... But..." Mark couldn't think of anything else to say.

"It's not only pigeons, you know," said his grandfather, which mystified Mark even more. It must have shown on his face, because his grandfather went on. "I'm talking about homing instincts," he said. "Pigeons have it. You let them go miles from home and they find their way back. Well, other things have it, too. Cats, of course. You often hear of people moving home hundreds of miles away, and the family cat goes missing, only to turn up back at the old house weeks later."

Mark began to think that where missing marbles were concerned, his grandfather had more than a little personal experience.

"But they're *animals*," he said. "They can sense things, like smells, or follow the stars, or something. Marbles are *things*. Things don't come back."

"Rubbish!" cried his grandfather. "What about boomerangs? What about hay fever? What about nightmares?"

Mark was speechless.

"All of those things can come back," his grandfather went on. "Why can't marbles? It seems to me that you take a terribly literal approach to the world, dear boy. Haven't you ever talked to your father? I've often said that science is stranger than fiction."

Mark tore his mind with an effort from the image of a boomerang following

his grandfather around a playing field, and decided to talk very slowly.

"Things can't just appear and then disappear," he said. "Where would we be if, for example, we were sitting here and the chairs suddenly disappeared?"

There was an awful silence for a moment, during which Mark found himself clutching the table just in case. But nothing happened.

"Of course, most things don't just appear and disappear," said the elderly man, "but how you know, young Mark, whether these chairs are still here the moment your back is turned is beyond me. Still, marbles are different. Did you know that the ancient Egyptians probably played marbles? The Romans certainly did. I think it's quite likely that cavemen played marbles, too."

"Dobblers!" said Mark.

"Exactly," said his grandfather.

"Anyway, something as ancient as that has to have special qualities, don't you think? It wouldn't still be around, if not, would it?"

Mark, who felt that he had long ago lost a grip on reality, tried hard to think of what Jumbo would say. Jumbo, as far as he knew, had never had an imaginative thought in his life. But Mark, who had had many, found that his brain had somehow ceased to work.

"Toast?" he asked, politely. "Or cereal?"

And his grandfather, perhaps wisely, dropped the subject.

Mr. Mack senior stayed for another two days, but the subject of round glass objects was not mentioned again. Only, as he hugged him goodbye, the old man said to Mark, "I'll check up on you-know-what when I get home. And if they're there, I'll send them back. Okay?"

"Okay," said Mark. He was tempted to wonder exactly how crazy old people had to be before they were taken away by men in white coats, but he remembered just in time that he himself had seen marbles disappear into thin air. This was probably just another subject, like alligators in sewers and bodies in the bath, that it was better not to think about.

That afternoon at school, Mark sat with Frizz and Jumbo as usual at lunchtime. The talk was of whether toads really have antifreeze in them (some do), why girls wear pink (some don't), and whether the school football team stood any kind of chance in the championships (some hope!)

Afterwards, Mark wandered across the playground to pick up his physics books. He looked at the school clock and was just thinking that his grandfather must be arriving home about now when ... *clunk!* ... something hit him hard on the head. And again, and again, and again!

Long after the jokes about Mark's missing marbles had faded from the memory of the school, the mystery of the returning marbles lingered on. But Mark, who more than anyone had the bruises to remind him, decided once and for all that there are some things on Earth that simply cannot be explained. He told his father this, that evening at supper, and for once that turned out to be a good idea.

"You're so right," said Professor Mack with feeling. "Why do you think I study distant planets? I can't help feeling that they simply must make more sense than this one."

You may not be surprised to know that Mark has since become an astro-physicist himself. It's odd, isn't it, that planets look strangely like marbles...

The
Musical
Mouse

Your first pet is special. Often, that's because of the amount of time it has taken you to persuade strangely reluctant parents to let you have a pet in the first place. Why is it that they can only ever see non-existent problems? When I asked my dad if I could have a lizard, he said, "No way. It will leave hair on the sofa." Oh yes? A *lizard*?

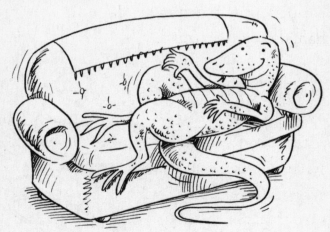

When I mentioned that I would quite like a hamster, Mum said, "That's all very well, Arthur, but I know who'll have to take it for walks when you're too lazy to get out of bed at the weekend. If you think I am going to be dragged around the countryside by a great, slobbering creature like that, you can think again."

Sometimes I think my parents come from prehistoric times. Maybe then giant hamsters stalked the earth. Quite possibly, they slobbered. I'm pretty sure it doesn't happen today. Anyway, I didn't get my hamster *or* my lizard.

I campaigned for a long time for a parrot. I liked the idea that it could talk to me and say rude things about certain people (need I say more?) who never listened to what I was saying. Then, one day at school, we learnt something useful. It's rare that you learn anything useful at that place, so I was pretty surprised. Mrs. Spangler told us that parrots had hugely powerful beaks, which I already knew really. I just hadn't thought what it meant. She said they could crack brazil nuts with one bite. Now, we'd just had a bowl of nuts for Christmas, and I can tell you that it would take a small steamroller to get into one of those things. The thought that a comparatively puny parrot could crack one with ease gave me pause for thought. Could it, for example, snap the tops off my favourite felt pens? Might it crunch into my models of the entire Italian football team? What exactly would happen if it decided to take a bite of a person's earlobe or big toe? The answers, I decided, were *yes*, *YES*, and *OWWWW!* I dropped my parrot campaign there and then. Since my parents hardly seemed to have noticed six long months of steady pressure, they didn't turn a hair (so to speak) when I suddenly began suggesting that a rabbit would really enhance our lives as a family.

"I completely fail to see how," said my father in his usual positive way. "Unless we could eat it when it was nice and plump. My mother often used to cook rabbit."

This was so gross, I could hardly speak. Mum was no better.

"Darling," she said, with her mind on one of her crossword competitions, "it will make a terrible noise, running round on one of those little wheels in the middle of the night. You won't get any sleep."

You see what I mean about parents? I tried hard to get them to understand that the hutch would be outside and there was no question of a little wheel. To be fair, my father did then come up with an almost-sensible objection.

"Arthur," he said, "has it occurred to you that we live on the fourteenth floor of a block of flats. Where exactly do you propose that we put this hutch? Hanging out of the window on a bit of elastic?"

I muttered a bit, but he was right. I pretty much despaired of ever getting a pet of my own right there and then. We're not actually supposed to have animals in the flats at all, because of the noise and mess. Frankly, our neighbours cause more noise and mess than a herd of elephants could possibly make. Mrs. Meliflua sings her ghastly opera at full blast on one side. Hairy Harris (that's not his real name, but it suits him) leaves bits of motorbike on the landing for people to fall over. When we first moved here, Dad did complain about both of them, but nothing happened except that Hairy Harris made several threatening gestures in our direction in the lift and put up a picture of a skull and crossbones on his door. Mrs. Meliflua puts her nose in the air whenever she sees us, which often results in her falling over a bit of motorbike.

Here's another of my observations on life coming up. One day, I'm going to write them all down in a book to save my own children the trouble of learning them by bitter experience themselves. It's this: it's just when you give up hoping for something that it comes along anyway. The very next day after the conversation about the rabbit, my father suggested that I might like him to buy me a mouse.

It was such a surprise that I didn't understand what he was talking about for a while.

"It wouldn't be much good without a computer," I said.

"Don't be a wally, Arthur," he said, "I don't mean that kind of mouse. I mean a little furry thing with pink ears."

"Look," I said, "I haven't played with soft toys for years. Everyone I know would laugh at me. Thanks all the same, but no thanks."

"Arthur, sometimes I think you're on a different planet," said Dad (as if *he* can talk!) "I mean a pet mouse. I mean a little scampering, scuffling thing with a twitchy nose, four feet and a tail. And, in case you think I haven't given this serious consideration, I plan to buy you a cage for it, too. I can't bear the thought of Mrs. Meliflua's screams if it ever escaped into her flat."

Well, I was speechless for a good minute (a record for me, as Dad was quick to point out). I hurried him into the lift before he could change his mind. The pet shop was only round the corner.

I'd been in the pet shop lots of times before, until the owner threw me out for drooling at the lizards and hamsters but never buying anything. He eyed me with a good deal of suspicion now, but Dad was already asking to see some mice, so I didn't have any trouble. At least, not that kind of trouble, but choosing a mouse was pretty difficult. They were all cute. I did try to persuade Dad that mice needed company, but he said I was lucky to get even one, and anyway, I would be its company. In the end, I chose a little white chap with a cheeky face and a way of putting his nose in the air that reminded me of Mrs. Meliflua.

"As long as that's the *only* way he's like her," said Dad, "I don't mind. It's bad enough having one opera-singer on the landing. We don't want two. Now, which cage shall we get?"

I'll say this for Dad, when he makes up his mind to do something, he does it thoroughly. He didn't just buy the smallest, cheapest cage. He said we had to be sure that Squeaky (that's what we decided to call the mouse. I know it's a bit obvious, but it seemed to suit him.) was comfortable. The cage we bought in the end was big enough for several mice. I did mention that, but Dad pretended not to hear.

Squeaky settled into his new home very quickly. He scurried about his cage in a way that made me pretty sure he liked it. He made himself a really cosy little bed in one corner and nibbled at the seeds and things I gave him with enthusiasm. After only a day, I couldn't imagine life without Squeaky. Even Mum and Dad seemed fond of him.

"Now remember," said Mum, when she had watched Squeaky doing his cute little face-washing act, "you absolutely must not take him out of his cage under any circumstances. If he got out into the hallway, who knows what would happen? I'm pretty sure that Hairy Harris would stamp on him and Mrs. Meliflua would probably scream the place down. Though nobody did anything about *his* mess or *her* noise, I bet they'd throw us out for having a pet before Mrs. M.'s screams had

died down. Luckily, she's away until the end of the month, or I'd have been worried about meeting her when we were bringing all this stuff in."

Over the next few days, I got to know my new friend a bit better. I discovered that he liked apple but not celery. I found that he always washed his ears when he woke up. He liked to run up and down the cage chasing his own tail but sometimes he would stand on two feet in the middle and

wave his arms about, almost as though he was conducting an orchestra.

And Squeaky was very good at night. He didn't run around on his wheel or make any kind of noise except a little bit of scuttling and some tiny munching sounds.

It was on Saturday that I found out about Squeaky's other talents. I cleaned out his cage, as I had promised Dad that I would do every single week, and was just watching him doing his standing-in-the-middle-of-the-cage performance when Squeaky started to sing. Yes, sing! I don't mean little squeaking noises that just might be singing, either. It was real music. The kind of thing that Mrs. Meliflua sings when she's in residence.

"*La, la, la, la, la, la, la, LAAAA!*" sang Squeaky, clasping his paws in front of him. I couldn't believe it. Squeaky took up another pose. "*Me, me, me, me, me, me, MEEEEEEEEEEEEE!*" he yodelled. It was amazing. It was extraordinary. It most definitely *wasn't* my sort of music. I edged closer to the cage, thinking that I might be imagining it. The sound grew louder and louder. I opened the window,

to be sure that it wasn't coming from there. Outside, a plane went past, a car hooted in the street, and those impossible kids from number twelve shouted as they skateboarded up and down the pavement. There was no grand opera to be heard.

I don't often consult my parents when I have a problem in life. It's been my experience that their advice is usually twenty years out of date. But in a situation like this, I didn't know which way to turn. I went into the sitting room, where Dad was watching the TV and Mum was about to paint her toenails, and begged them to come and see Squeaky. Something in my tone must have alarmed them, because they both assumed straight away that he was lying in the middle of his cage with his legs in the air.

"No, no!" I said. "He's fine. But he's doing something very odd."

I held my breath as we went into my room. You know how it is if your tooth aches and you go to the dentist? It stops aching the minute you get into the waiting room. I was afraid that when we went back, Squeaky would be doing mouse-like things without an aria to be heard. But for once, the unexpected did happen. Or didn't happen, depending on your point of view. There was Squeaky, standing just as I had left him, and singing his heart out.

"It's unbelievable," I said.

"It's extraordinary," said Dad.

"It's Mozart," said Mum. And she started to sing along with Squeaky. My Mum's not very tuneful and she doesn't sound a bit like Mrs. Meliflua, but I could tell that she knew the tune. Squeaky really was singing Mozart. And he was a mouse. And he was in a cage in my bedroom.

We all sat down on my bed. It was partly so we could think and partly because our knees felt a bit wobbly.

"Do you think we're having some kind of halucination?" asked Dad. "What did you put in that sausage and mash last night, Pru?"

"There was nothing wrong with it," said Mum sharply. She's a bit sensitive about her cooking, probably because she's got a brother who's a chef and acts as though there's no one else in the world who can turn out anything edible.

"It could be that genetic engineering," I suggested. "I saw a programme on TV where they were growing a human ear on a mouse. It was horrible. Maybe they've started growing human vocal chords on them now."

"I think human vocal chords would look as weird as an ear on a mouse," said Mum. "I mean, I think you'd be able to tell. They'd stick out or something."

"I think he *is* getting fatter," I said. "But I thought it was because he liked our food better than the stuff he was getting in the pet shop."

We might have gone on worrying about it for weeks if there hadn't been a knock on the door at that moment. Mum and Dad didn't seem to be able to move,

so I went to answer it. To my surprise, Mrs. Meliflua stood on the doorstep.

"Ah, Arturo," she said (she always talks like that), "are your parents in?"

I led the way to my bedroom and showed her Mum and Dad sitting on the bed looking weird.

"Are they ill?" asked our neighbour.

"No," I said, without thinking. I guess I'm just a naturally truthful person. "They're a bit shocked because my mouse has started singing Mozart."

"Mouse?" said Mrs. Meliflua, her voice rising to singing pitch. I could have kicked myself. In the heat of the moment, I'd completely forgotten about the no-pets rule. But Mrs. Meliflua had moved on from the mouse problem.

"Did you say Mozart?" she asked, going up to the cage. "Good heavens, you're right! It's *Le Nozze di Figaro*."

"Is it, indeed?" said Dad.

"And what's more, I know where it's coming from," said Mrs. Meliflua.

"So do we," said Mum. "It's Squeaky."

"It most certainly is *not* squeaky!" cried our neighbour. "It's the very best equipment that money can buy. That's what I came around to tell you. Firstly that I'm back and secondly that I have bought a new music centre and earphones so that you will no longer have cause to complain when I play my opera."

"But we thought you sang it!" cried Dad. "Do you mean that Squeaky's cage is acting as a kind of receiver?"

"It sounds like it," said Mrs. M., flattered that we had taken her for a great singer. "And no doubt it will do the mouse good, especially in her condition."

Well, yes, it turned out we did need that bigger cage after all. It's just as well we're friends with Mrs. Meliflua now!

The Missing Mummy

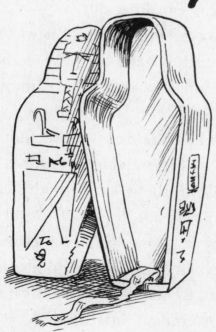

Mrs. Morris looked worried. She sighed several times as she tucked Millie and Max into bed.

"What's the matter, Mum?" asked Millie. "I'll clear up the mess in the bathroom tomorrow, honestly."

"It's not that, pet," said her mother. "It's just that something is bothering me at work. I can't make it out."

Max frowned. He knew that his mum found it hard to make ends meet, and her job as a cleaner at the museum meant a lot to her. She could only clean at nights, when the doors were shut to the public, so Mrs. Evans from next door always came in to sit with the children while she was out.

"Is it something we could help with?" asked Max. "We're good at solving mysteries. Remember how we found your watch for you at Christmas?"

Mrs. Morris had lost her precious watch, one of the last presents the twins' father had given her, on Christmas Day. After interrogating everyone (there was always a houseful at Christmas), Max and Millie decided that the watch must be among all the wrapping paper from the presents. Sure enough, after half an hour of delving and diving and making a huge mess, Millie had spotted the watch at the bottom of the pile.

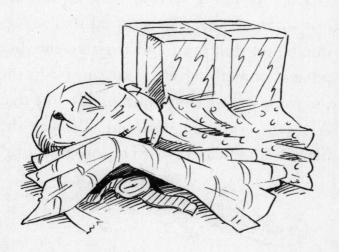

Mrs. Morris smiled.

"You're both great detectives," she said, "but this is a grown-up mystery. You see, no one is supposed to be in the museum at night, except me. But just recently I've found that things have been moved *after* I've cleaned them but before I've gone home. That means there is someone else moving around the museum when I am. I've never seen anyone, but I know that must be so. Alf, the security guard, has never seen anyone either. It's not so much that I'm worried that some-one could jump out and frighten me, but what if something went missing? I'm the only one with a key. I'm the only one that Alf sees going in and out. I'll get the blame. And I can't afford to lose this job."

"You should report it to the museum manager," said Millie. "At school, we always have to tell the headteacher if we see something bad or strange. You should do the same. Then they'll know it's not you."

Mrs. Morris looked a lot happier.

"You're absolutely right, Millie," she said. "Clever girl! I'll pop in after I've dropped you both at school tomorrow and see the manager myself. Now, lie down, both of you. Mrs. Evans will be here any minute and I've got work to do."

"You'll be careful, won't you, Mum?" said Millie.

"If there's anything scary, hit it with your mop!" advised Max.

"Goodnight!" laughed their mum.

But Mrs. Morris didn't go to see the museum manager the next day because she didn't come home that night. Mrs. Evans waited until she was quite sure that something was wrong. She tried ringing the museum, but the phones were all switched off for the night. Then she rang the police. They promised to go round to the museum straight away to see what had happened.

Alf, the security guard, was sitting at his post just inside the front door.

"We're looking for Mrs. Mary Morris," the first policeman explained. "We understand that she works here."

"Oh yes, I know Mary," replied Alf Gardner, "but you'll find her at home now. She left over an hour ago. Look, this is where she signed herself out in the book. Here."

"The signature looks pretty shaky to me," said the second policeman. "Was she okay when she left here?"

"Oh, she was in a hurry," said Alf. "She always likes to get back to her kids as soon as she can. But she does a good job, mind you. The old place has never looked as clean and well-kept as it does these days. I can give you her address, if you like. I've got it here somewhere."

But the policemen exchanged a glance and said goodnight. They already knew where Mrs. Morris lived, and they knew that she wasn't home. Carefully, they retraced her path through the dark streets, but there was no sign of the missing woman at all.

As soon as he saw Mrs. Evans getting breakfast in the kitchen next morning, Max knew that something was wrong.

"Where's Mum?" cried Millie.

Mrs. Evans decided that it was best to tell the truth.

"You mustn't worry, my dears," she said, "there's probably a very good reason why your mother hasn't come home. Maybe she stopped to help someone who was hurt. You know what she's like. And she hasn't been able to get to a phone to let us know."

"Mum would always let us know," said Max, suddenly sounding much older than he looked. "Something's happened to her and we need to speak to the police."

"I've already done that, dear," said Mrs. Evans. "They're looking into it right now. They'll soon find her, I'm sure."

"No, I mean that Millie and I have important information," said Max. "I'm going to call them myself, right now. Mum showed us how to do it, didn't she, Millie? Come on!"

It wasn't long before Max and Millie were telling the story of their mother's worries to the police.

"That's very interesting," they were told. "We'll make enquiries straight away."

But a couple of hours later, the police called at the house.

"I'm sorry, kids," said Sergeant Fox. "The security guard says he doesn't know anything about any prowler at night. He reckons your mum never mentioned it to him. Do you think maybe she kept it to herself until she was sure?"

"Maybe," said Millie doubtfully. "But I'm pretty sure she meant that she'd discussed it with this Alf. He can't be telling the truth!"

"He's worked there for twenty years," said the policeman, "and there's never been so much as a teaspoon missing. I think he's pretty reliable. He's coming up to retirement age. I don't think he'll do anything to put his pension in danger. Do you have any other ideas?"

Max and Millie looked at each other. They did have ideas, but they didn't want to share them just yet.

"Mrs. Evans is going to stay with you until we find your mum," said the policeman. "Try not to worry. It's not as easy as all that to lose a whole grown-up person. We'll find her."

As soon as the police had gone, Max and Millie went to sit in their treehouse and discuss their next step.

"I don't know about you, but I don't like the sound of this Alf character," said Max. "I'm sure Mum talked to him. If there *was* an intruder in the museum, then Alf isn't doing his job properly. Or maybe he's letting someone in. And if there isn't anyone coming into the museum, then the person moving things around has to be Alf himself. Either way, he's involved in this somehow."

"I agree," said Millie, "and the other thing I think is that we've got to go over there and have a look around. We can't find out anything staying here. And you know, Mum said we were good detectives herself. Let's slip out tonight."

Late that night, Mrs. Evans put the twins to bed and told them for the twentieth time not to worry. It was a silly thing to say, really. Of course, they were worried. But they knew they would feel a whole lot better as soon as they started *doing* something about it.

It wasn't difficult to creep out without disturbing Mrs. Evans. The poor woman had hardly slept the night before and was now stretched out on the sofa in the living room, snoring gently.

Max and Millie hurried through the deserted streets towards the museum. If they saw anyone coming, they scurried into a shop doorway. At last, the great big doors of the museum loomed above them at the top of a flight of steps.

Millie and Max peered cautiously through the windows in the doors. They could see Alf, the security guard, sitting at his desk reading the paper and drinking a cup of coffee.

"He's not paying much attention to the monitors on his desk," hissed Millie. "Anything could be going on and he'd never notice."

"Let's hope that's true," said Max. "Now, remember that loose basement window Mum told us about? Come on!"

It wasn't long before Max and Millie were inside the museum. Although many of the lights were on, it still seemed very dark and different at night. The twins had been there lots of times during the day, looking at interesting exhibits that their mother had talked about, but there had always been people about and excited chatter in front of the main display cases.

"What should we do?" asked Millie.

Max looked uncertain, too.

"I'm not sure," he said. "I think we should just walk around and look out for anything that's out of place. We know these galleries well enough. We should notice. But we'll have to be careful to look out for the cameras that send pictures to Alf's monitors."

"That's easy," said Millie. "They're in the same place in each room, and what's more, they are set for people a lot taller than us. If we work our way along the wall in each gallery, they won't be able to spot us."

"Then let's get going!" whispered Max. "I think we should stick together, don't you?"

"That's probably a good idea," agreed Millie, hoping she sounded as though she didn't mind too much either way. She really didn't want to be on her own in this spooky building.

Everything seemed to be in its place in the costume gallery. Although they looked rather ghostly at night, the models in their costumes and the suits of armour at the end all looked untouched.

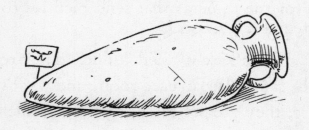

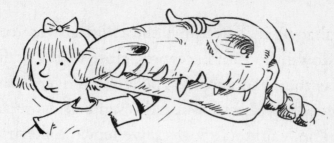

It was the same story in the gallery where the Greek and Roman finds were kept. The vases, bowls and piles of coins stood silent and still.

In the gallery with prehistoric remains, massive dinosaur fossils looked as they always did. For the first time in their lives, Max and Millie didn't stop to gaze and gasp at them. They had more important things to think about.

As soon as they entered the gallery with ancient Egyptian displays, Millie stiffened and stopped.

"There's definitely something different here," she hissed. "Don't you feel it?"

Max nodded.

Very carefully, the children moved down the room, keeping close to the wall as they had agreed. The stones covered in hieroglyphics looked the same as always. The cabinets with jewellery, make-up boxes and little statues seemed fine, too. But in the centre of the room, something was dreadfully wrong.

In the middle of the floor there always stood a huge wooden casket, taken from an Egyptian tomb. It was beautifully decorated, with gold and precious stones, and showed the calm face of a pharaoh, his arms crossed in front of him. Many times when they visited the museum, Max and Millie had discussed whether there was a mummy inside the casket. Now they wondered even more, for the casket was open, its great lid swung back on its hinges to show the dark and empty inside—and a single piece of bandage.

"D-d-d-do you think there was something inside it?" asked Max.

"Y-y-y-you mean, something that's out here with us now?" stammered Millie. "I don't know. I really wish I did."

"In any case, this proves that there's something going on," said Max, feeling a little better now he knew that Millie was as frightened as he was. "I'm sure this isn't meant to be open. But why hasn't Alf noticed? I'm more suspicious of him than ever. Isn't he supposed to do rounds or something, so that he can make sure everything is all right all the way through the museum? Shhhh! I think I can hear him coming now! Let's hide behind this cabinet. Quick!"

The children were only just in time. Thudding footsteps echoed through the gallery, coming closer and closer. Millie peeped out from their hiding place and clamped her hand over her mouth so that she wouldn't scream.

"Is it Alf?" whispered Max.

"No. Yes. Maybe!" Millie had never sounded so frightened. Max peeped out himself and gasped. Lumbering towards them down the gallery was a huge mummy. Ancient bandages covered him from head to foot. There were dark holes where his eyes should have been. His great arms swung stiffly by his sides. And he seemed to be heading straight for the twins' hiding place!

Millie felt rather than saw the huge shadow fall over them. Very, very slowly she raised her eyes and looked straight into the mummy's fearsome face.

But Max, still looking at the mummy's feet, saw something even more breathtaking. Peeping out from under the bandages, he was pretty sure he saw a glimpse of dark blue uniform. Quick as a flash, he lunged forward and grabbed a loose piece of bandage around the mummy's ankle, pulling and pulling as hard as he could.

Max had only meant to see if the bandages came away, but his move was even more successful. Wrapped up in his stiff bandages, the mummy found it hard to keep his balance. As Max pulled, his feet slipped out from under him and he fell, banging his bandaged head on a carved stone.

"Ow!" The mummy said a few very unpleasant words that were definitely not ancient Egyptian. Millie raced forward and tied the loose bandage to the leg of a cabinet. Max did the same with the other leg and the two arms. There was no way that the mummy could move now.

Max's face was grim as he seized the bandages around the mummy's head and pulled them away. A familiar face appeared.

"Alf Gardner!" cried Max. "I knew it! What have you done with our mum?"

Alf spluttered and spat.

"Interfering brats! Why couldn't you leave things alone? Your mother was just the same. Always asking questions and interfering. I'll be retiring in a few weeks time and do you know how big my pension will be? Not enough for a flea to live on! I was just going to help myself to one or two bits and pieces to make me comfortable in my old age. I should have known you two would take after your mother."

"Where is she?" Max was talking through clenched teeth. "What have you done with her?"

"Oh, she's okay," said the guard. "Another day and I would have been gone. Then you'd have found her, safe and well. She's shut up in the storeroom at the end of the prehistoric gallery. Trussed up with all the old bones in there."

But Max and Millie were off before he'd even finished speaking.

"Mum! Mum!" yelled Millie, heaving open the storeroom door.

"Mmmmmfnnng!"

Inside, Mrs. Morris was bound and gagged. Her eyes filled with tears as she glimpsed her children.

"Oh my dears," she cried, as Millie tore the gag from her mouth, "I thought I'd never see you again. How worried you must have been. I'm so sorry!"

But the twins were crying, too, so relieved that they couldn't speak.

"Hey, untie me!" laughed their mother. "How can I hug you trussed up like this?"

The police shook their heads when they heard how Millie and Max had taken matters into their own hands, but they were impressed, too. So was the museum manager.

"It seems to me that you've a lot to offer us," he told Mrs. Morris. "Brains and bravery run in the family. How would you feel about becoming our Head of Security? There would be a big rise in salary, of course. When could you start?"

"As soon as you like," smiled Mrs. Morris. "With two great detectives like this to live up to, I'd better get some practice right away!"

The Hidden Homework

Mrs. Closter looked even more severe than usual—and that's really saying something. She has a face like an unripe lemon at the best of times.

"You know what I'm going to ask you, Angela," she said. "But I can only guess at your reply. *Where is it?*"

Angela gave a charming smile.

"My homework, Mrs. Closter?"

"Absolutely," the teacher confirmed.

"Well," said Angela, smiling again, "it's the most extraordinary thing."

"I don't doubt it." Mrs. Closter's tone could have sliced ham.

"You see," Angela was getting into her stride now, "my little cousin Hugo came to stay yesterday and he's only just learning to use his potty. Unfortunately…"

"Stop right there!" cried Mrs. Closter holding up a magisterial hand. "I think we can all guess where this is leading, and I think I speak for the whole class when I say *we don't want to hear it*. The gist of the matter, as usual, is that you have failed to give in your homework. Last week, the dog ate it. The week before, a mysterious fire in your home burnt only the homework and nothing else at all. Before that, we had a freak hurricane in your garden, a strange mould growing in your bedroom, and a hamster who needed a nest."

"It's very odd, isn't it?" Angela gave an unconvincing giggle. "These things don't happen to my homework for any other classes. It's only maths homework. I can't imagine why."

"My guess," said Mrs. Closter coldly, "would be pretty simple. My guess would be that if a certain person hasn't actually *done* her homework, it's much more likely that some extraordinary disaster will befall it. What do you have to say about that?"

"I really don't know, Mrs. Closter," said Angela sweetly. "You see, I *always* do my homework."

Now this, as you have probably guessed, was not strictly true. Angela always did her geography homework, her history homework and her English home-work. She almost *never* did her maths homework. The reason, as you have probably also guessed, was that Angela was not very good at maths. She didn't understand what she was supposed to do most of the time. Here Mrs. Closter must be held at least partly to blame. She was an excellent teacher for the brightest and best pupils in the class, but she had very little time for those who were less confident. She tended to think they weren't trying or were lazy instead of realizing that they simply had lost track of what she was saying about fifteen minutes earlier.

Over the weeks that followed the explanations for missing homework that Angela came up with became more and more extraordinary.

"My granny used it to light the fire," she said one week.

"My mother had new covers put on the sofa and unfortunately my homework was lying on a cushion," she tried.

"My dad borrowed it to read on the train and left it in the luggage rack," was another suggestion.

Pretty soon, Mrs. Closter made a point of enquiring into the health of Angela's homework as soon as she stepped into the class.

"How's the homework, Angela?" she would ask. "Eaten by an alligator? Made into jam by your granny? Caught up in a tidal wave and washed all the way to Japan?"

Angela would shake her head, but in truth her own explanations were only slightly less fantastical.

It was just at this point that a new girl joined the class. Her name was Clara and she turned out to be extraordinarily good at maths. Of course, she became Mrs. Closter's favourite at once.

"Does anyone know the answer to problem three?" the teacher would ask. "Robert? Damian? Angela? No, I thought not. Now, Clara, perhaps you can tell us."

And Clara always could.

You might think that Clara's maths abilities would make her unpopular with the rest of the class, but the opposite was true. This was partly because Clara was a jolly, fun-loving girl who tried to make friends with everyone. However, it was mainly because Clara regularly helped everyone with their homework on the bus on the way to school.

Strangely enough, although Clara was nice to everyone, she soon became special friends with Angela. It wasn't long

before Clara asked Angela about the famous missing homework mystery.

"Those things don't really happen, do they?" she asked.

"Well, only in a sort of a way," said Angela evasively.

"Shall I take that as a 'no'?" smiled Clara. "So why don't you just do the homework? It wouldn't take that long."

"Oh but I do!" cried Angela. She had been telling stories about it for so long that she could hardly bring herself to stop.

"No, you don't," said Clara firmly. "What I want to know is, why not?"

Angela hung her head. It was hard to confess, even to a friend. At last she managed to whisper the problem.

"I don't understand the questions, usually," she said. "Then I'm scared of getting the answers wrong. I'm pretty sure Mrs. Closter would laugh at me."

"Well, you could be right about that," said Clara grimly, "but, you know, there's nothing very hard about maths. Why don't you let me show you one or two things? It's easy—really!"

After an hour or two of explaining some simple problems to Angela, Clara began to have a little more sympathy for Mrs. Closter. Angela had got the idea so firmly into her head that she didn't understand maths, she very often didn't even try. However, Clara was not a girl to give up easily. Day after day, she took Angela off to a quiet corner at lunchtime and showed her the mysteries of maths. Very, very slowly, Angela began to see what she was talking about. At last the day came when Clara started to explain something and Angela said, without thinking too hard about it, "No, no, I already know that. The answer is $a + b$."

Clara laughed, fell back in mock exhaustion and said, "At last! My work is done! How about having a go at that homework tonight, Algebra Angela? It didn't look too difficult to me."

"Well, it wouldn't, would it?" said Angela. "But I'll give it a try. Let's meet before class in the morning and you can check what I've done."

"Sorry," said Clara. "I'll have to see you in class. I've got another five maths-muddlers to help before school."

That night, Angela tackled her homework and found it nothing like as frightening as she had feared. She looked with pride at the neat rows of figures in her exercise book.

"If Mrs. Closter's got a weak heart, I may be about to change our maths classes for ever," said Angela gruesomely.

Next morning, when Mrs. Closter called for homework to be handed in, Angela went up with all the rest and added her exercise book to the pile. Mrs. Closter, weak heart or no weak heart, noticed right away and at once dived on the pile of books and extracted Angela's.

"Ah ha!" cried the teacher. "I am holding in my hand an extremely rare item, notably a piece of homework from Angela Sparkes Rogers. It deserves to go into the school museum, to be enjoyed by posterity, but instead I am simply going to mark it. Now, let's look, which page is it on, Angela?"

"The last one," said Angela, trying hard to sound polite. Mrs. Closter made her madder than any other person she knew. It was at times like this that she remembered why.

Mrs. Closter turned to the last page and grew very red in the face.

"Is this your idea of a joke?" she spluttered, shaking the book in the air. "What happened, Angela? Surely you didn't run out of excuses, did you?"

"What do you mean?" Angela looked surprised and bewildered. But since she had been pretending surprise and bewilderment in Mrs. Closter's class for the last six months, it didn't impress the teacher one bit.

"Perhaps you'd like to find it for me," said Mrs. Closter, handing Angela the book. "The homework, I mean."

Angela turned confidently to the last used page and then stared. That wasn't her homework! Desperately, she began

$$57 + 135 - 72 \div 3 = 40$$

$$\begin{array}{r} 7 \\ 14 + \\ \hline 21 \end{array} \qquad Z + Y = 2X \qquad \begin{array}{r} 77 \\ 18 - \\ \hline 59 \end{array}$$

leafing through, but the homework wasn't there at all.

"I'm sorry," she gasped. "I think I must have put it in another exercise book. I have done it, honestly. I'll look when I get home. I'm sure I'll find it. I'll give it to you in the morning."

"Well done, Angela," replied the teacher in a voice heavy with sarcasm. "You've managed to find another way out of the homework trap. I wondered what you would do when you couldn't think of any more excuses. This is good, very good. I expect your English teacher is really pleased with you. I would guess that your imaginative writing is first class.

If only the same could be said about your maths! Go and sit down."

Angela went back to her seat with a frown on her face. At lunchtime, after an accusing look from Clara, she promised her friend that it was true. She *had* done her homework, but she must have brought the wrong exercise book to school. That evening, when she got home, Angela searched in vain through every exercise book she could find, even the ones labelled "Poetry" or "Spanish verbs".

There was no sign of the maths homework. Angela began to worry that she had imagined doing it in the first place. She decided to take precautions next time.

When Mrs. Closter handed out homework the next time, Angela took Clara home with her and made her watch while she did the homework in front of

her. Clara thought this was taking things a bit far, but she duly noted that Angela had finished all six questions and which notebook she had written them in.

"Now I want you to take the book," said Angela, "so that I don't lose it accidentally between tonight and maths class tomorrow."

"That's ridiculous!" laughed Clara. "How could you possibly lose it? But if you insist, I will take it. See you in the morning, maths maniac!"

But Angela didn't see Clara in the morning. It seemed that she had been taken ill with a bad cold during the night and wouldn't be back in school for the rest of the week.

"So, Angela," said Mrs. Closter, "have you done your homework?"

"Yes, Mrs. Closter," said Angela with absolute truthfulness.

"Then where is it?" screeched Mrs. Closter. "I'm fast losing my patience with you, young lady. Oh, Clara has it, does she? How very, very convenient for you. You will stay behind after class and do some extra questions during breaktime. This ridiculous state of affairs simply cannot go on."

It *was* a ridiculous state of affairs, and it got worse. Next time, Angela gave her homework to her mum to keep overnight. Her mum, at the end of a long and tiring day, put it in the washing machine with Angela's brother's dirty jeans. Very little of the blue-and-silver-covered exercise book survived.

A week later, Angela did her homework before she even left school and put the exercise book in her locker to be picked up in the morning. Naturally, the caretaker had to choose that very night to check the lockers for all the doorknobs and coathooks missing from the school. In the process, Angela's exercise book tumbled out of the locker and into the caretaker's bucket of soapy water. Another fine mess.

"You know what I think?" asked Clara. "I think it's fate getting its own back on you. As soon as the scales are equal, your homework will stop going missing. Don't worry."

But Angela did worry. After all, she remembered all the many times when she had "mislaid" her homework before. She, more than anyone (except, of course, Mrs. Closter) knew that she had a long way to go before the score was even.

But, strange as it may seem, the very thing that was driving Angela mad, also proved to be her saviour. For one sunny afternoon, after interrogating Angela about the homework that the juggernaut outside the school had run over (yes, really!), Mrs. Closter finally lost her icy composure—and when she lost it, she really lost it!

The headmaster came to see what all the shrieking about and persuaded Mrs. Closter to go home and rest. No one was very disappointed when, later in the term, the class was told that Mrs. Closter had decided to retire and would not be returning.

It can't have been a coincidence, can it, that the same afternoon, five of Angela's exercise books suddenly began to overflow with the answers to problems? Her homework was hidden no more.

The Surprise Trip

Zooooooooom! *Crash!* It was the kind of sound that was heard several times a day in the corner house on Barrett Street—especially during the long summer holidays.

"Annie! My favourite vase!" Mrs. Corbett was not impressed. "Can't you girls be just a little bit more careful?"

"Sorry, Mum!"

"Sorry, Mum!" chorused the girls, but a moment later they were dashing about just as dangerously as before.

Mrs. Corbett retreated to the kitchen where her husband was hiding behind his newspaper.

"Can't you say something, George?" she asked. "We won't have anything left that isn't smashed, bashed or covered in pink paint at this rate."

"Mmmmnnnng," said Mr. Corbett. To be fair, he had never been terribly good at disciplining his daughters. When they were tiny and poured porridge into his slippers, he couldn't bring himself to shout at them. They had been naughty, of course, but they looked so sweet with their little golden curls and winning smiles. Later, when they were old enough to answer back, George Corbett found that he was doomed in any argument he embarked upon. His girls were smart—there was no doubt about it—and one way or another they had him beaten from the day they were born. Luckily, Mrs. Corbett was made of sterner stuff, although even she found it hard to handle the girls these days—especially during the long summer holidays. Now!

The day wore on, as days do, and the whole family retired to bed at last. Mrs. Corbett flopped back on to her pillows, exhausted. For once, her husband didn't have his nose in the paper, and there was a moment of peace and quiet to talk.

"Seriously, George," she said, "I don't think I can survive a whole summer of this. What are we going to do?"

"Darling, you're just tired," said her husband. "Annie and Cara are not so bad. No worse than other girls of their age, I'm sure. It's just high spirits, that's all. You wouldn't want them to be little mice, sitting in a corner with a book all day, would you?"

Mrs. Corbett was getting ready to say that there was, surely, a middle ground between mousiness and mayhem when a ghastly noise rent the night air. It sounded like a hippopotamus being dragged backwards through a kitchen-equipment shop.

"Wha ... Wha ...?" Mr. Corbett leapt out of bed and picked up a pillow to defend himself. In the process, his wife unfortunately ended up on the floor. The noise stopped as suddenly as it had started. There was an eerie silence.

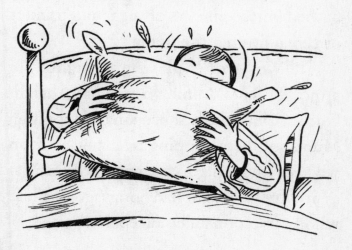

Mr. and Mrs. Corbett's first thought was for their daughters, but the girls' room was empty.

"Why am I not surprised?" muttered their mother, grimly gathering her dressing gown around her as she crept down the stairs, her husband close behind.

The scene in the kitchen was hard to take in all at once. Two little girls and a dog sat in the middle of the floor with saucepans on their heads. Yes, the dog, too. All around them, broken plates, bashed saucepans, jars of sugar and packets of cereal littered the floor.

"We were playing knights in armour," said Annie in a small, bright voice. "Only these saucepans are too big, Mum, and kept slipping over our eyes, so we kept knocking into things." She said it as if Mrs. Corbett had long ago made a wholly irresponsible saucepan-choice.

"I can see that," replied that woman, leaning weakly against the door frame, "but there's something else I don't understand."

"Oh," said the girls, and looked a little guilty.

"Woof!" said the dog, and hung his saucepan-sized head.

"Exactly," said Mrs. Corbett, "and I'd like you to feel free to chime in here, George. Annie, Cara, whose dog is this?"

"Ours!" cried the girls.

Sometime later, when the girls, protesting loudly, had been returned to bed, the kitchen had been returned to some kind of order, and the dog had been returned to a very relieved pensioner at the house opposite, Mr. and Mrs. Corbett sat down at the kitchen table and had a Council of War over a cup of tea.

"Even you must see," said Mrs. Corbett, placing her hand firmly on the newspaper that her husband was about to pick up again, "that we can't go on like

this. I thought we only had to go through the sleepless nights stage when the girls were babies. It looks like I was wrong. Now, what on earth are we going to do with them for a whole summer so that we are all sane at the end of it?"

"Emigrate?" suggested Mr. Corbett gloomily. "The girls, I mean. We could stay here."

"If only," sighed his wife. "But wait a minute, that gives me an idea. What about sending them so stay with friends or relatives for a week or two? It would just give us a break before we needed to face the fray again."

"Good plan!" Mr. Corbett looked brighter already. "Now, where could they go?" He thought furiously. "My sister Jane and her family?" he suggested.

Mrs. Corbett shook her head. "You've forgotten the incident with the

barbecue last summer," she sighed. "Although how you could forget that your children set fire to your sister's house, I'm not sure."

"Hmm, maybe they wouldn't be so keen. You're right." Mr. Corbett thought some more.

"How about your brother and his two children? The girls have always got on well with Jack and Jenny."

"After the rabbit accident?" asked his wife.

Mr. Corbett shuddered. "I don't want to talk about it," he said. "How about your parents, then?"

"George! My mother is seventy and has a bad heart. My father is seventy-two and has high blood pressure. Do you really think that Annie and Cara would be good for their healths? How about *your* parents, though?"

Mr. Corbett considered. Mrs. Corbett considered, too.

"They're always saying they'd like to see more of the kids," said the former.

"They're pretty fit and healthy," said the latter.

"They live *two hundred miles* away!" they shouted together. "They're *perfect*!"

Mr. and Mrs. Corbett retired to bed looking happier than they had for days.

It took only a few anxious minutes on the phone the next morning to sort out all the arrangements. Mr. Corbett, steeling himself for the ordeal, undertook to drive the girls up to their grandparents the next day. Mrs. Corbett launched herself into a frenzy of washing and ironing to make sure that everything was ready in time. The girls, remembering that Gran and Grandad Corbett lived near the seaside, decided to practise their sandcastle-making in the garden. There wasn't any sand (don't ask), so they used soil instead. Mr. Corbett came out later to find that his prized begonia bed was now a kind of ditch and a small version of Mount Everest stood in the middle of the lawn. It just shows how firmly he had fixed his mind on the prospect of a daughterless few days that he merely smiled and said, "Very nice," when the girls showed it to him.

The journey north the next day was just as bad as Mr. Corbett had expected. Annie was sick twice. Cara got lost at a service station. The car was pulled over by the police because the girls were making rude gestures out of the window. Two pieces of luggage were discovered to have been left behind, but Mr. Corbett was adamant. There was no way he was going to turn around until he had deposited his passengers with their grandparents.

Mr. Corbett almost had qualms when he saw the dear, trusting faces of his parents looking out eagerly for his arrival. How could he do this to the pair who had lovingly bathed his knees when he fell over and helped with his homework? Mr. Corbett forced his mind to consider the electric guitar he had been refused when he was thirteen and the truly dreadful embarrassment of seeing his father dancing at school parties. His heart hardened.

"Mum! Dad!" he cried. "Here we are! I'm sorry I can't stop long, but I have to be back by six."

"Never mind," said his mother. "It's these girls we really want to see!" She hurried forward to hug Annie and Cara.

Mr. Corbett, feeling a little hurt, decided that his parents deserved all they got and climbed back into the car. For seven blissful days, he could look forward

to peace and quiet. He could hardly believe it.

Cara and Annie were on their best behaviour that evening. Mrs. Corbett's cooking was a lot better, they agreed, than either their mum's or their dad's. Her cakes, in particular, were outstanding.

"Wheaweooauhee?" asked Cara, her mouth full of cake.

"She means, 'When can we go to the beach?'" Annie translated.

"Well, tomorrow, of course!" said Gran. "We've had lovely weather all week."

But—and for once the girls really couldn't be blamed—later that evening the weather turned colder. Dark clouds filled the skies. A vicious wind began whipping at the waves and sneaking around street corners. By the morning, the weather was about as unpleasant as it gets in the middle of winter. The girls looked out of the window in disgust.

"What are we going to do now?" they groaned.

"I'm sure the sun will come out later," said Gran. "How about helping me to do some baking?"

The girls cheered up at once. They spent a happy morning in the kitchen, making more mess than old Mrs. Corbett would have thought possible, and enjoying themselves hugely.

After lunch, however, there was no sign of the weather improving. There was some talk of a bracing walk along the pier, but no one felt very enthusiastic. Besides, the girls' waterproofs were in the luggage that had been left behind.

Finally, Grandad produced some board games and a riotous game of snakes and ladders ensued. The girls introduced their grandparents to a version of the game where moves had to be acted out all over the furniture—climbing up chairs or slithering down a kind of chute made from sofa cushions.

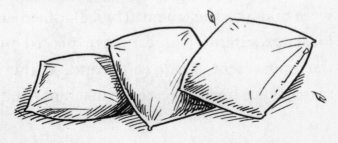

Later, after putting the girls to bed and spending over an hour sorting out the furniture in the sitting room, the Corbetts sat down to watch the weather forecast. It wasn't good. In fact, even more rain, wind and cold was foreseen for the next seven or eight days.

"Whatever are we going to do with two lively girls for a whole week cooped up in here?" asked Mrs. Corbett, showing that she had more in common with her daughter-in-law than either of them could have imagined.

"I'll have a think about it," said her husband. "I'm sure there are lots of things to do in town."

So, for the next three days, the girls were taken to the cinema (twice), dined at local restaurants (three times), played in the amusement arcade (only once as they managed to break one of the machines and the manager banned them for life) and tramped around the local museum (also only once after an unfortunate incident with a stuffed polar bear).

By day four, everyone was feeling pretty fed up.

That evening, when the girls were safely in bed (it was lucky that their hosts didn't know just how unsafe "safely" could be in this respect), the Corbetts sat down, exhausted and anxious.

"I can't imagine what we're going to do tomorrow, Ted," said Mrs. Corbett. "Those girls are on the go all day. I'm not sure I can survive another couple of days."

Mr. Corbett was leafing through the local paper.

"Hey," he said, "look at this! There's a mystery coach trip leaving at nine in the morning. It lasts all day, and if we could get tickets, it would solve one day at least."

"What's a mystery coach trip?" asked his wife. "Will it be scary?"

"No!" laughed her husband. "The mystery is where you are going. They take you somewhere nice, but they don't tell you where. When you get there, you usually have a few hours to look around, get something to eat and so on, and then you come home again. It would be perfect. And we might even see some sun."

Next morning, the girls were keen, the trip wasn't fully booked, and Mr. and Mrs. Corbett looked forward to a couple of hours dozing in their seats. The coach left on the dot of nine, just as advertised.

As their grandparents dozed, Annie and Cara chatted to other passengers, made faces out of the window at other children on other coaches, and played endless games of I-Spy.

Mr. and Mrs. Corbett woke with a start when the tour guide called out.

"We're almost at our destination, ladies and gentlemen," she said. "You have four hours to look around and visit the sights. Please be back at the coach by three o'clock sharp."

Mr. and Mrs. Corbett looked out of the window with interest. They were not even sure which direction they had been travelling in.

"Now, I wonder where we are," said Mrs. Corbett. "Oh!"

"Oh!" echoed her husband.

"Oh!" cried the girls. "We're home! Look, there's our house!"

It was true. Of all the places in all the country the coach had brought them back to the picturesque little town where the girls lived.

"Anyone fancy a cup of tea?" asked Mrs. Corbett. "I think I know where we can get quite a good one."

Mr. Corbett shifted uneasily as they stood on the doorstep of his son's house.

"I'm not sure they're going to be glad to see us," he said.

But later, when explanations had been given and tea drunk, the girls parents looked at each other and smiled.

"A few days on our own has been lovely," they said, "but it's been much too quiet. It's great to see you home again!"

Vanishing Vera

Mike didn't usually read the paper. He thought it was a grown-up thing full of boring business news and other stuff he wasn't at all interested in. But for the past week he had been the first to pick up the paper in the morning and often disappeared into the bathroom with it so he wouldn't have to fight his father for the opportunity to read it first. He was fascinated, as many of his friends at school

were, by the story that had dominated the news for the past week and a half. It concerned the mysterious disappearance of Elliot Z. Jakes, master magician and illusionist.

The facts were perfectly simple. While staying with a friend in a chalet in the mountains, Elliot Z. Jakes had taken to going on long walks by himself. His friend reported that he seemed unhappy and talked often of the pressures that being so famous created. He was tired, he said, of not being able to walk down the street without being pestered by fans who wanted his autograph, his trademark multi-coloured scarf, or the secrets on which he had based his career. The friend pointed out that it was these fans who had given Elliot Z. Jakes the wealthy and lifestyle that he so much enjoyed. But the illusionist still seemed upset. The friend hoped that his time in the mountains would give Elliot a chance to rest.

The night before Elliot Z. Jakes disappeared there was a heavy snow-storm. The two friends sat in their chalet talking about old times, when they had been at school together. Elliot went to bed early, saying that he wanted to be up early to prepare to return to his home. He felt, he said, much better and knew now what he had to do to get his life back on track.

Next morning, Elliot's friend awoke to find that the illusionist had already left the chalet. His bags were neatly packed and labelled in the hall, but of the famous magician there was no sign. The friend assumed that he had gone for one last walk before asking for a lift to the station with his bags.

He was wrong.

When Elliot had not returned to the chalet by lunchtime, his friend became worried. When the afternoon passed and

darkness began to fall, he became so alarmed that he called the police. But it was too late that night to start searching the mountains. Instead, checks were made to see if anyone had left the area by train, plane or car that day. Several people had, of course, but none of them sounded at all like Elliot Z. Jakes.

The next day, at first light, the search resumed. It wasn't long before, in the untouched snow in front of the chalet, a set of footprints was picked up. Their size matched the boots and shoes in Elliot's packing. The trackers followed the footprints up the mountainside for several miles. Then, as suddenly as they had appeared, the prints disappeared. In the middle of a snowy wasteland, where no other footprints or marks of any kind were to be seen, the footprints suddenly stopped. There was no sign that the snow had been disturbed, but still the only thing that the rescue team could think of doing was to dig. But they found nothing. Apart from the footprints, there was nothing to show that Elliot Z. Jakes had ever been there.

Although these discoveries were reported on the day after the magician's disappearance, and the story ran for weeks, this was really a triumph of the journalists' ability to make a very few

facts stretch to a lot of words. There were
interviews with Elliot Z. Jakes' magical
assistant, his hairdresser, the man who
made his magic wands and his old mother,
who lived in Tennessee. There was nothing
more to say about *how* the illusionist had
gone missing. The police investigated
every sighting of the missing man from
Brazil to Brighton, but all of them turned
out to be perfectly ordinary people going
about their ordinary business. Elliot Z.
Jakes had apparently disappeared from the
face of the earth, leaving not a trace.

This was the story that Mike was following so avidly in the bathroom each morning, while his father and his sister Ellen hammered on the door with various needs of their own.

Mike had his own ideas about how the magician's last great illusion had been achieved. He was less sure about why. If Elliot Z. Jakes had wanted to retire, why hadn't he just returned to one of his palatial mansions around the world and stayed there? It doesn't take long for the public to forget someone who has been terribly famous if he or she just stays at home and doesn't do anything. After all, no star would need to pay for lots of publicity if being a star was enough by itself to ensure that fans queued on your doorstep every morning. Perhaps, thought Mike, it was simply professional pride that had caused the master magician to make his final act a particularly spectacular one. "Always leave the audience wanting more," Mike's drama teacher used to say. In this case, the public certainly did want more.

While Mike was still avidly reading every line he could lay his hands on about the mysterious disappearance, Aunt Vera came to stay. She was a very, very old lady—not Jake's aunt, or even Jake's dad's aunt, but Jake's grandad's aunt. But she was as spry as she was sharp.

"Now, what's this you're reading, Mike?" she said the morning after she arrived. "An old woman like me doesn't have a bladder of steel, you know."

Mike blushed. He really didn't think that old people should go around talking about bladders. Well, he didn't think that anyone should go around talking about bladders. It just wasn't something you wanted to hear about before your breakfast—or after it, come to that.

Mike told Aunt Vera about the missing magician.

"Poo!" said his aunt rudely. "I can think of dozens and dozens of ways it could have happened. I don't know why everyone is making such a fuss about it."

"Such as what?" asked Mike. "I was thinking of a helicopter myself."

"Not a bad idea, young Mike," said Aunt Vera. "But wouldn't the rotor blades blow the snow about? You'd probably see blurring of the footprints nearest to the site of the disappearance."

Mike was impressed that his aunt knew about rotor blades. As if she could hear what he was thinking, Aunt Vera said sharply, "I'm just old, Mike, not stuck in the Dark Ages. I have heard of helicopters, you know."

"I've thought about the rotor blade problem myself, actually," said Mike. "I would guess that if Elliot Z. Jakes was winched up to the helicopter on a really long line, so that the helicopter could stay high, then the snow wouldn't be disturbed. At least, not more than could be accounted for by a light wind. I looked up the weather for the region, too, and there *was* a light wind that day."

"Good work," said Aunt Vera, "but I think my ideas are more exciting. How about a hot-air balloon? It wouldn't disturb the snow at all, as long as it didn't land."

"I thought about that, too," said Mike, "but it's hard to believe that anyone would *plan* to escape in a hot-air balloon. They're just not very easy to manoeuvre. And the weather can be a problem, too. A friend of mine had a flight booked with his granny and it was cancelled three times because the weather was wrong. And it's so terribly noticeable and not as quiet as

people think. There's one that comes over here sometimes and the gas-burners make a terribly loud noise."

"All right, not a balloon then. Your reasoning is good, young Mike," said his aunt, "although I still think a balloon is a lot quieter than a helicopter. Now I shall have to tell you my own favourite theory. An eagle!"

"An eagle?"

"Yes, a big one, obviously. It could swoop down, clutch Elliot Z. Jakes in its

powerful claws and carry him off without leaving a trace."

Mike had so many objections to this that he hardly knew where to start.

"Are there eagles that big?" he said, as a beginning.

"There are eagles that can scoop up monkeys," said his aunt, "and, I don't know if you know this, but Elliot Z. Jakes was a remarkably small man."

"Still, you couldn't *train* an eagle to come and pick you up," said Mike.

"Who said anything about training? Maybe it was just one of those things that happened out of the blue. There's not a scrap of evidence to suggest that Elliot *planned* to disappear."

"I suppose not," said Mike slowly. "But, well, wouldn't they have found … er … bits of him by now?"

"Not if the eagle has a nest high up in the mountains," smiled his aunt. "Don't look so worried, Mike, I don't seriously think that magician was seized by a giant bird. And yes, I do think he planned to disappear. I never liked that man. I always thought he looked too full of himself when I saw him on TV. I think he's quite definitely responsible for all this and I also think he's enjoying every minute of it."

"So how did he do it, then?" asked Mike. "Have you got any more good ideas?"

"Better than that," said his aunt. "I'll *show* you how it was done. And what's more, I know exactly where the little weasel who caused all this fuss is right now."

Mike looked impressed, but he didn't really believe her. She looked mysterious when he pressed her further and told him that he would see tomorrow.

The next morning, two things made Mike forget all about the missing magician for a while. The first was the fact that it snowed during the night and kept snowing the next morning. It was the first snow of the season in that part of the world, and Mike was very excited. Even better was the fact that Mike's friend Ellen came back from visiting a distant cousin. She arrived, laughing and covered with snow, halfway through the morning.

"It's supposed to stop by lunchtime," she said. "Then we can go outside and play. It's the kind of snow that sticks together, so we can make a snowman."

Aunt Vera was dozing in a corner. She opened one eye when she heard this and smiled to herself.

The family had lunch together and, sure enough, just as they were finishing, the snow stopped and the sun came out. Mike and Ellen leapt up from the table at once, but Aunt Vera held up a hand.

"I know you want to be getting out there," she said, "but I wonder if you could just wait a minute. I'd like to walk down to the end of the garden and I'm not so steady on my feet these days, especially in the snow. I just need to go and … er … powder my nose, but I'll be back in a minute. I only need to walk down to the gate and back, just to get a bit of air."

The children felt slightly impatient, but of course they said, "No problem." Aunt Vera shuffled off to … er … powder her nose.

Ten minutes later, when she hadn't returned, Mike's mum looked a little concerned and said, "I do hope she hasn't got stuck or anything. I'll just pop up and see what she's doing."

She came down again a few seconds later looking flustered. "She's not in the bathroom and I've checked all the bedrooms," she panted, "but she's nowhere to be seen. "She didn't come back into here, did she?"

Everyone shook their heads. Another search of the house was carried out. Ellen even looked in the cupboard under the stairs and got bumped on the nose by a mop, but of Aunt Vera there was no sign.

"Maybe she forgot she asked us to wait and went out by herself," suggested Mike. He was dying to get outside. "Come on, Ellen! Let's go and look."

There was no sign of Aunt Vera in the front garden. The even, untouched snow stretched down to the road. Ellen and Mike ran round to the back and at once stopped in their tracks.

Leading from the back door was a set of footprints, looking distinctly as if they could belong to Aunt Vera. They meandered, step by step, into the middle of the lawn. And stopped.

Mike looked down in astonishment.

"I don't believe it," he said. "She told me she would show me, and she has!"

He looked all around, to see if there was a place that the old lady could have jumped to. But the flowerbeds showed no signs of disturbance and were five metres away in all directions. Surely a ninety-year-old woman couldn't make jumps like that? Besides, it was clear that the foot-prints were made by simple walking, not

with the kind of force needed to launch yourself halfway across a garden. Mike looked long and hard at the footprints but he couldn't for the life of him think how she had done it.

"So where is she?" asked Ellen. "She can't have just disappeared into thin air."

"I don't suppose she can," said Mike, "but in any case, I don't think we'll have to wait long to find out. If I know Aunt Vera, she'll want to show how clever she's been. And, to be fair, I want to know, too. Let's go back into the house for a minute and wait."

Although Ellen protested about the snowman she had planned, Mike insisted. Although he didn't think that Aunt Vera would make her surprise last all afternoon, he wasn't quite prepared for hearing her cheery greeting as he went back into the kitchen.

"Hello, my dears!" she called from her comfortable chair in the sitting room. "I'm sorry I forgot you were waiting for me. As you saw, I didn't get as far as the gate after all."

"All right," replied Mike, "I give up, how did you do it? And where is Elliot Z. Jakes?"

"Do you really not know? It's the oldest trick in the book, Mike. I simply walked backwards in my own footprints."

Mike laughed, then frowned.

"Yes, but that means you're back here. Elliot isn't back in the chalet. They would have looked."

"Isn't he? What about this friend he's supposed to be staying with? I don't suppose anyone even noticed him when Elliot was around. And anyone who can manage magic can manage a little make-up and a false beard. My advice to the police would be to question the so-called friend. From what I could see of Elliot Z. Jakes, he wasn't a man that anyone would want to be friends with."

Aunt Vera was right, of course. Elliot announced his trick to the press the following week. He got lots of publicity, naturally, but I hear that he still doesn't have a friend in the world...

Mrs. Duke's Diet

Tilly was a good-natured girl in most ways but she was bossy. Already, at the age of six, she thought she knew better than all the other children she knew and most of the adults, too. Her own close family, consisting of her mother, her father and her granny, who lived with them, was already fed-up with Tilly's high-handed ways.

One morning, her father found her sitting outside the bathroom with a stop-watch and shaking her head.

"What on earth are you doing, Tilly?" he asked.

"You only brushed your teeth for fourteen seconds, Dad," said Tilly. "That's not enough, you know."

Dad scuttled off down the stairs, rather pink around the ears.

The same week, Tilly explained to a visitor in clear and ringing tones that her mother brushed dust under the carpets when she was in a hurry.

Tilly's mother giggled nervously and offered the visitor more coffee and Tilly a considerable bribe to go to her bedroom and stay there.

But it was Tilly's beloved granny who suffered the most. Tilly had over-heard her mother saying that granny was getting forgetful. She now felt it was her duty to remind Granny about everything, whether she needed it or not.

"Your glasses are on your nose, Granny," she would say, helpfully.

"You haven't finished your tea, Granny," she would mention, when the poor woman, who certainly had all her wits about her, had just taken a first sip.

In vain, Granny tried to reassure Tilly that she didn't need a nursemaid, but it was hard to get rid of Tilly's attentions unless she found a new victim. Luckily for Granny, this turned out to be Mrs. Duke next door. It was not so lucky for poor Mrs. Duke.

It happened like this. One day when Granny was out, Tilly's mum invited Mrs. Duke for lunch. It was only sandwiches and coffee, but the neighbours liked to get together from time to time to swap news and keep up with the local gossip. Tilly played quietly in the background, but she was listening to every word.

Mum passed Mrs. Duke a plate of sandwiches, saying, "Prawn or cream

cheese, Daphne? I know you like both. Just help yourself."

But Daphne Duke hesitated.

"Oh, Sandra, I shouldn't really. I've ... er ... got to watch what I eat at the moment." And she patted her stomach.

Tilly's mum grinned and leaned nearer to her neighbour, with a glance at Tilly. The two women lowered their voices and whispered together for a few minutes, before Tilly's mum went into the kitchen and came back with more sandwiches for her visitor.

Tilly was annoyed at not being able to hear, but she knew what Mrs. Duke was talking about anyway. Tilly's mum was frequently trying to lose a few pounds. She would sit at the supper table, gazing mournfully at the mashed potato or pushing away the pudding.

"I mustn't," she would say.

It was obvious that Mrs. Duke was going on a diet. She was, Tilly thought, a bit plump anyway. There and then Tilly decided to try to help her. Mrs. Duke often picked Tilly up from school when Tilly's mum was busy, so there would be lots of opportunities to keep an eye on what Mrs. Duke was eating. Tilly, who had often found her mother with her head in the fridge and a guilty look about the parts of her that were visible, knew that dieters needed watching.

With this new interest in life, Tilly abandoned her surveillance of Granny (much to that lady's relief) and began a serious campaign on Mrs. Duke. She found that she had lots of opportunities.

The very next day, Tilly and her mum came across Mrs. Duke in the local supermarket. Mrs. Duke had a trolley piled high with all kinds of goodies. There were lots of packets of Malted Munchies, for a start, which was a kind of biscuit that Tilly particularly hated. She also knew that her mother never ate biscuits when she was on a diet. While the two women discussed the contents of their trolleys ("I just can't get enough of them," laughed Mrs. Duke), Tilly did a little rearranging of her own. She carefully removed all the packets of Malted Munchies and replaced them with bags of carrots and broccoli. She also confiscated two large pizzas, a big

bag of pasta and a packet of doughnuts with caramel icing.

Mrs. Duke finally waved goodbye and went off to finish her shopping. Tilly and her mother did the same. But at the check-out, Tilly's mum ran forward in concern as she saw Mrs. Duke holding a bag of carrots in one hand and scrubbing her eyes vigorously with a tissue in the other hand.

"Whatever is the matter?" cried Tilly's mum. "What can I do?"

"I'm fine," sniffed Mrs. Duke. "They do say your brain shrinks and mine certainly has. I've bought lots of things I don't want at all and I don't even remember doing it. I mean, Frank and I don't even *like* carrots!" And she burst into tears again.

Tilly's mum, giving her daughter a sharp look, comforted Mrs. Duke and ran around the store for her picking up the things she really did want. She wasn't very surprised to find a little pile of them tucked behind a soft-drinks display.

On Monday, Mrs. Duke picked Tilly up from school, as often happened. Less usually, she was in the car, although the school was only a fifteen-minute walk from Tilly's house.

"I'm feeling so tired at the moment that I didn't feel up to walking," Mrs. Duke explained. "Oh, look, there's the headteacher. I must just have a quick word with her. You stay there."

Tilly frowned. She knew that it was very important to take lots of exercise if you wanted to lose weight. Going in the car was no good at all. What could she do? Quick as a flash, Tilly pulled out the keys that Mrs. Duke had left in the ignition and dropped them down the nearest drain. When Mrs. Duke came back and started hunting feverishly through her bag and the door pockets of the car (stuffed full of empty Malted Munchies packets), Tilly didn't say a word. It is one thing to take a diet seriously, quite another to own up to trying to keep someone on the straight and narrow.

In the end, Tilly got her wish, of course. Mrs. Duke was forced to take the little girl firmly by the hand and walk her back home.

"I'll go back and pick the car up when Frank comes home from work with the other set of keys," she said, "but what I've done with them mystifies me. I really do think I'm losing my faculties some days. Dear me."

"Is it old age?" asked Tilly, smiling sweetly up at Mrs. Duke.

"Good grief, not yet!" laughed her neighbour, but the laughter was a little forced, Tilly felt. Still, she was glad that she had forced Mrs. Duke to do a little more exercise. Every little helps.

Back at home, and rather pink in the face, Mrs. Duke suggested that Tilly might like a drink of juice, while she made herself a cup of tea.

"And I've got a bag of doughnuts here," said Mrs. Duke. "There are just two left. Can you get the plates out for me, please, Tilly?"

Tilly got the plates out while Mrs. Duke made the drinks. The little girl was thinking furiously. Didn't Mrs. Duke have any willpower at all? Doughnuts could not possibly be a good idea.

As she brought the teapot and the juice to the table, Mrs. Duke asked Tilly to put one doughnut on each plate. Tilly took a big bite out of hers right away, just because Mrs. Duke wasn't allowed them, it didn't mean that Tilly wanted to miss out. Then, while Mrs. Duke was fetching the milk, Tilly quite deliberately dropped the other doughnut on the floor.

"Oh dear," she said. "I am sorry. I'm afraid you won't be able to eat it now it's been on the floor." This was what Tilly's mother had always told her.

But Mrs. Duke had been eyeing the doughnut with great eagerness as she got the drinks ready. She eyed it with even greater eagerness now as it sat on the floor.

"Oh, the floor's pretty clean and I think if I just brush the sugar off...," she began, bending stiffly to pick up the longed-for snack.

But Tilly was too quick for her. She stepped forward and stamped one foot firmly on to the doughnut, squirting jam all over the kitchen. Mrs. Duke, halfway to the ground, let out a squeal of horror.

"Tilly! What are you *doing*?"

She looked up into the little girl's face. The two exchanged a long look. Mrs. Duke knew that Tilly had mashed her doughnut deliberately. Tilly knew that Mrs. Duke knew. But Mrs. Duke felt very silly to have wanted the doughnut so desperately.

"Never mind," she said briskly. "Perhaps you'd like to help me clear up all this mess, Tilly."

Tilly, to be fair, did help. But she found that Mrs. Duke did not look at her in such a friendly way for the rest of the day. And she looked out of the window as Tilly munched her way with satisfaction through her own jammy treat.

One way and another, Tilly was pretty satisfied with the way her campaign was going. Over the next week or so she successfully prevented Mrs. Duke from eating several sausage rolls, a large slice of cherry cake, another packet of Malted Munchies, and some chocolate drops meant for the dog! She did not know that Mrs. Duke, unable to fulfil her cravings when the little girl was around, indulged in several treats by herself during the day.

Tilly was nothing if not determined. She pursued her campaign until the end of term. Then, during the summer holidays, when she was at home all the time and Mrs. Duke kept an eye on her more often while Tilly's mother was working, Tilly stepped her mission up a gear. She took to raiding Mrs. Duke's fridge for goodies and claiming that she wanted to eat them herself. Several times, she caught a look of quiet desperation on her neighbour's face, but Mrs. Duke always gave in to avoid a scene. Tilly knew by instinct that her neighbour was wary of upsetting a child who might cry inconsolably if pushed too far or denied too much. By the middle of August, Tilly definitely had the upper hand and knew it.

But Tilly was distressed to find that Mrs. Duke was not getting any thinner. In fact, the reverse was true. She was getting very large indeed, especially around the middle. Tilly noticed that her neighbour had had to buy some special clothes to wear as her old ones wouldn't do up any more. Where was she going wrong?

At the same time, as Tilly regularly cleared cakes and cookies from Mrs. Duke's fridge and store cupboards, the little girl herself was growing quite plump. Like Mrs. Duke, her clothes no longer fitted, and her mother had to take her into town to buy some roomier items.

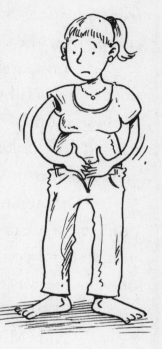

It was during one of these trips that Tilly finally found out why Mrs. Duke wasn't losing any weight. The reason came as a terrible shock to her, although it probably won't to you. The revelation came when Tilly's mother, searching for larger sizes for her daughter, paused in front of some baby clothes and started cooing over the tiny trousers and tops.

"Oooh, aren't these gorgeous!" she said. "Look, Tilly! We'll have to get some of these soon."

Tilly looked at her mother with growing horror.

"I thought you knew," she said. "I don't *want* a baby brother or sister. I told you that and you said it was okay because one like me was enough for any family."

"What are you talking about, Tilly?" said Mum, frowning. "*I'm* not going to have a baby. Mrs. Duke is! Surely you've noticed how fat she's been getting? That's the baby, growing inside her."

"But she's on a diet," said Tilly. "She doesn't want to be fat. Does she know about the baby? I don't think she'll like to have one. She doesn't like me very much."

Tilly's mother dealt with all this one point at a time. She explained that ladies who are going to be mothers have to be very careful what they eat, because some things aren't good for the baby. And yes, Mrs. Duke did know about the baby and she was very, very happy about it. As for not liking Tilly, of course she did, although Tilly could be quite difficult sometimes and, she had heard, rather a greedy girl.

I'd like to be able to say that Tilly was a reformed character after making such a big mistake, but I'm afraid I can't. What I can say is that she went off cakes and biscuits rather rapidly and was soon a shadow of her former self. She is looking forward very much to taking the new baby in hand as soon as it is old enough. Luckily, this is a fact of which the baby is as yet blissfully unaware.

Haunted
Hyssop
House

Detectives have to be nosy. There are just no two ways about it. If you are not curious about *what* people do and *why* they do it, it is no good considering a career as a private eye.

Jackson Jones was determined to be a detective when he grew up. He thought is was probably best if he started now, while he was still young. He was pretty sure there were all sorts of skills that he could develop so that when he finally launched himself upon an unsuspecting world as Jackson Jones Investigations, he would quite simply be the best.

But Jackson already had the biggest qualification for being a detective—he was the nosiest boy you ever met. And on one occasion at least, this was his downfall.

Jackson had been watching old Mrs. Davies down the street for some time. Jackson himself called it surveillance. Mrs. Davies called it spying. She was a woman who kept herself to herself. Not for her the morning gossip over the fence with her neighbours. She rarely had visitors and hardly ever went out. Jackson had heard his parents talking about their shy neighbour. To his mind, her behaviour was far from normal. He decided, for no very good reason, that the reason she was so seldom seen out and about was that she had something to hide. He was determined to find out what it was.

As a matter of fact, Mrs. Davies was a great scholar. Her passion in life was

deciphering Egyptian hieroglyphics. She wasn't interested in people today very much at all, but she was very interested in people who lived over two thousand years ago. She spent day after day, and very often night after night, poring over ancient texts.

It didn't occur to Jackson Jones that Mrs. Davies had better things to do than shopping and gossiping, but if it had, I'm afraid his behaviour would have been the same. He was simply curious by nature.

Once he decided to begin watching Mrs. Davies, Jackson equipped himself in a methodical manner. He bought a new blue notebook and wrote on the front of it: "Subject X". He didn't think it was professional to use the subject's real name on what he called a "dossier". Next the boy-detective borrowed his father's best binoculars (Mr. Jackson was a keen bird-watcher) and tried out all the front-facing windows in his house to see which gave the best view of Mrs. Davies' front door. Luckily, the best window was in his own bedroom. Jackson would be able to watch night and day if he wished. Finally, he went to the shops and bought himself a bag of surveillance provisions. Jackson was a boy who liked his food and he found that long hours of watching could be even more tedious if he didn't have a bag of drinks and munchies close at hand.

At last, when everything was ready, Jackson opened his new notebook on the first page and wrote, "Day 1: Thursday

1st September: 0800 hours" at the top. His long vigil had begun.

But Jackson was about to have a very frustrating time. Although Mrs. Davies very rarely came out of her front door, she did have to get food and other necessities like anyone else. A couple of times a week, she set off with a little basket on wheels to buy what she needed.

But Mrs. Davies was a woman who had all her wits about her. The first time she left the house after Jackson's regime had begun, she looked up and noticed a boy staring at her through partly-drawn curtains. It was odd, but she thought no more about it.

Later, when she returned from her shopping, Mrs. Davies happened to look up again. The boy was still there. Hmm.

It didn't take Mrs. Davies long to realize that it wasn't only when she went

out that the boy peered out from behind his curtains. She did a bit of peering out herself and saw that he sat, hardly moving except to reach into a bag by his side, hour after hour and stared at her house.

Mrs. Davies felt a little disturbed. It wasn't, she felt, natural for a boy of any age to be sitting still in a darkened room. Boys should be out and about, running and jumping and generally making a big nuisance of themselves, she thought.

Then there was the question of her privacy being invaded. Mrs. Davies had nothing to hide from anyone, but no one likes to live as if they are in a goldfish bowl. She found the whole situation far from comfortable.

After two weeks, things took a turn for the worse. Jackson decided that the data he was collecting was simply not good enough. Page after page of his notebook was filled with such rivetting and vital observations as: "Subject X did not leave house. Subject X not visible. Subject X's movements unknown."

Jackson decided that he must get closer to his subject. He didn't mean that he should invite her for tea and try to get to know her. He meant that his position of surveillance should be a lot nearer to her house, so that he had a chance of finding out exactly what she did inside.

Now, Jackson's activities were impolite, unneighbourly, almost certainly downright criminal and, in the case of what he did next, extremely stupid.

One evening, as dusk was falling, Jackson crept down the road, flattening himself against the walls and railings of the gardens as much as possible (and thereby, I'm afraid, making himself a lot more conspicuous than he would otherwise have been). When he reached Mrs. Davies' house, he very, very carefully pushed open her creaking gate.

Now Mrs. Davies was old and not very steady on her feet, but her eyes and ears were as sharp as ever. She had watched Jackson's curious behaviour since he had left his own front garden a few minutes earlier. Now, she watched with horror as the weird boy began to crawl across her front garden on his hands and knees. What on earth did he think he was doing? He looked ridiculous.

Meanwhile, Jackson felt that he was making some progress at last. Inch by inch, he reached the front of the house and wiggled himself through a flower bed beneath a downstairs window. Then, very, very slowly, Jackson raised his head above the windowsill and looked inside.

It was at this point that Mrs. Davies finally felt she had had enough. The boy was a nuisance, even if he hadn't yet done anything really awful. Mrs. Davies made

up her mind to confront the snooper herself. She hurried over to the window and
flung it open ... *smack!* ... into the face of
Jackson Jones, Investigator.

Jackson fell back into the flower
bed and saw little coloured stars buzzing
around his head for a good five minutes.
As his vision cleared, he became aware of
two things: a horrible pain in his nose and
the sight of Mrs. Davies leaning over him
and looking very concerned.

"I do hope you're not badly hurt, my boy," she said. "Can you get up?"

Jackson wiggled each of his limbs in turn and decided that nothing was broken. As a conclusion, it was wide of the mark. Later that evening, in the casualty department to which Mrs. Davies had insisted on taking him, he was told that he had a broken nose.

"Broken?" gasped Jackson. He had not seen himself in a mirror since Mrs. Davies had thwacked him with the frame of the window. He had visions of his nose being squashed flat against his face.

"Don't worry," said the doctor. "Your beauty will be unmarred. I'm going to pack your nose with cotton wool and put a dressing on the tiny cut across the bridge. After two weeks, you'll be fine. Until then, you'll have to breathe through your mouth."

For a couple of days, Jackson's nose was a little tender when touched but was otherwise fine. The main difference that Jackson and his family noticed was that he lost all interest in food, even the contents of his bag of specially selected surveillance provisions. At first he couldn't understand it. Then he realized that his sense of taste had almost gone. Why on earth would breaking his nose make his taste buds give up? It was Jackson's small sister who solved the mystery when she found her brother toying with a plate of chips.

"You'll get your appetite back when the cotton wool comes out of your nose, Jackson," she said. "You need a sense of smell to taste things properly. With your nose bunged up, you can't expect to be able to taste. I'm surprised a great private eye like you doesn't know that. I learnt it in school last year."

Jackson was relieved but annoyed to be shown up by his own sister. He retired to his room to sulk and think about things.

Sitting in his room reminded the young detective of his ill-starred project to find out about Mrs. Davies. But he was smiling with satisfaction, considering that he had, after all, succeeded, even if it had turned out that Mrs. Davies was doing nothing illegal. The price of a broken nose was a high one, admittedly, but on his return from hospital, Mrs. Davies had invited him into the house. There, he had been fascinated to see the hieroglyphics she worked on, painstakingly deciphering their meanings.

"It's a bit like detective work, I suppose," she had said, with a sly grin at young Jackson.

Despite the "success" of his last case, Jackson did not want to wait for long before taking on a new project. Luckily, one presented itself almost at once.

The following morning, as the family gathered for breakfast, Jackson overheard his parents talking about Hyssop House. This was an imposing building on the other side of the street. It had been lived in by the same family for thirty years, but had recently been let—four times! Each family only seemed to stay for a few weeks—a month at most. Then the house became available again.

"The last lot only lasted ten days," said Jackson's mum. "No wonder there's a rumour that the house is haunted."

Jackson's dad gave a snort of laughter. "Well, that's one way of putting it," he said.

All of Jackson's detective instincts were aroused by this exchange. What was the secret of the house where nobody stayed? Was it really haunted or was there an even more sinister reason? Jackson's imagination ran riot. He imagined that the house was the base for a vicious gang of international smugglers. Each time a new family moved in, they were forced to move out—until they could "persuade" the family to move on again.

Jackson couldn't wait for the meal to be over. He had preparations to make!

Later that morning, armed with a new yellow notebook marked "Location X", a tape measure (for trying to find secret rooms and hidden passages) and a couple of cans of juice (instead of his usual bag of provisions), Jackson set off for Hyssop House. He had tried to borrow his father's camera, as well, but his dad was still smarting from the fact that his best binoculars had been returned with half a flower bed obscuring the lenses.

Jackson made his way cautiously down the drive. As he entered the gate, the passing postman called out.

"You're a brave man to venture down there!" and pedalled on his way.

Thrilled that he had been seen as an intrepid explorer, Jackson crept on. He found that entering the house was no problem at all. The last occupants had left without even closing the front door!

Inside, Hyssop House looked very much as you would imagine an abandoned house to look. It wasn't rotting or falling apart. It simply looked uncared for. There

was also evidence to show that the last family had left in a hurry. A teddy bear, a couple of shoes and even a

half-drunk mug of coffee stood in odd corners. Jackson was delighted. Here at last was a real mystery. One that he could get his teeth into. It might be the making of his reputation as a detective.

For the next two hours, Jackson roamed the house, writing down every clue he could find. They were clues that seemed completely unrelated, but the boy-detective knew that in the best stories, a keen mind could often see the pattern behind apparently random signs. Why, for example, was so much food left in the larder? Why did there seem to be an enormous number of tubs, cans and bottles of cleaning materials?

Back at home, Jackson puzzled over the information he had retrieved. It seemed to make no sense. There was, he was sorry to see, no evidence at all that the house was used by a gang of international smugglers—not unless they were evilly smuggling disinfectant, which seemed pretty unlikely.

For the next two weeks, Jackson returned again and again to Hyssop House. He searched every inch of it over and over again. From the mail that was still being delivered, he was able to work out the names of the four families who had most recently lived there (although his mother could have told him this if he had asked). Further than that, Jackson felt that his mission had been a failure.

He was still feeling depressed about it when he visited the doctor to have the cotton wool removed from his nose.

That afternoon, after a lunch that he had enjoyed for the first time in a fortnight, Jackson returned one last time to Hyssop House. As soon as he went in, he gasped and staggered back. A smell of overwhelming disgustingness filled every room. He could hardly breathe. No wonder no one could live here!

Jackson staggered home, gulping great lungfuls of pure air.

"I see you've been to Hyssop House," said his mother. "Why no one has fixed the drains in all this time, I can't imagine. It's a disgrace."

Jackson reluctantly felt that he was the disgrace—as a detective. He wondered if it was too late to consider a change of career, and whether Mrs. Davies would consider teaching him all she knew about Egyptian hieroglyphics...

The New Aunty Jane

Molly was pretty sure that people had it all wrong about aliens. They tended to think of them as little green creatures with funny heads and big, goggly eyes. Molly's reasoning was that if the aliens were clever enough to get here in the first place, surely they were clever enough to disguise themselves as humans—unless they were pretending to be cats or floorcloths, of course. The main point was that they would, if they had any sense at all, do their very best to be as inconspicuous as possible. After all, if you're an alien on a fact-finding mission, you don't want everyone screaming at the sight of you.

Now Aunty Jane could not be said to be inconspicuous in any way. From her glossy blonde hair to her long red finger nails, everything about her was designed to make as many people as possible look admiringly in her direction. So why was it that Molly became so convinced her neighbour was an alien from outer space? This is going to take some explaining…

For a start, Aunty Jane wasn't a real aunty, but she had lived next door to Molly's mum and dad since the little girl was born, so she was a sort of honorary aunty. She swooped down at Christmas and birthdays, smelling strongly of her favourite perfume, and presented girly gifts to her honorary niece.

Even from babyhood, Molly wasn't very impressed by girly gifts. She turned up her button nose at pink rabbits, lacy dresses and dolls in frilly pinafores. Red and yellow things that made a lot of noise were much more in her line.

But Aunty Jane was determined that Molly should be as feminine as she considered herself to be. Year after year, she persisted with the pink ribbons and the sparkly bracelets until the day came when Molly, aged about six, suddenly began to take an interest in them.

For a couple of years after that Aunty Jane became Molly's very favourite person. The little girl's parents became sick of hearing Aunty Jane's words of wisdom being quoted to them at every hour of the day.

"Aunty Jane says a lady never goes to bed without wearing perfume," said

Molly as he put on her pyjamas one night before bed.

"Aunty Jane never does anything without wearing perfume," said her mother. "But little girls smell very nice just as they are. Perfume is something you don't need until you are much older."

"But Aunty Jane isn't very old," Molly protested. "She told me."

"How old is not very old?" asked her mum, amused.

"I don't know," said Molly. "Aunty Jane says you must never ask a lady her age. But she's not as old as *you*, Mum. She hasn't got grey bits in her hair, for a start."

Molly's mother snorted and hurried her daughter off to bed. She felt she was being noble in not expressing her own views on the subject of Aunty Jane's age.

But the next day, at supper, Molly raised the subject herself.

"I was right, Mum, about Aunty Jane's age," she said. "She's only thirty-eight and you are forty-two!"

Molly's mother, who was in the middle of drinking a cup of tea during this announcement, had to get up to find a cloth to clear up the mess.

Molly's father paused with a large forkful of spaghetti swinging dangerously in the air.

"I wouldn't want to be ungallant," he began, "but…"

Molly's mum interrupted quickly with "More spaghetti, darling?" and reminded her husband under her breath that anything said in their house was bound to be carried by a certain person with a little button nose straight to the house next door. It took all her self-control, however, to keep to this resolution a moment later when Molly added to her announcement.

"Aunty Jane says she's really sorry for you, Mum, being so old. She's not looking forward to her fortieth herself. I told her not to worry. She looks so pretty it doesn't matter at all."

Molly's mother made a sound like a strangled warthog and hurried into the kitchen. It probably was as well that she was unable to see her husband, scarlet with laughter, choking on his pasta.

Things went on like this for some time, and Molly certainly never thought that her neighbour wasn't a perfectly human person. It was only after Aunty Jane returned from her holidays that the little girl began to have doubts. It was all very mysterious.

For a start, Aunty Jane was away for four weeks, which was quite unknown for her. Also, there was the fact that she didn't seem completely sure where her holiday was.

"A few weeks in the Bahamas is just what I need, Molly," she had said, "to restore my spirits after our depressing winter. These cold winds are ruinous for the skin."

But later the same week, as Molly watched her doing her packing, Aunty Jane sighed and said, "I'm so looking forward to my stay in Jamaica. Sun, sand and sleep will set me up for the year."

Molly didn't like to say anything. After all, anyone can make a mistake, but later she wondered why, at different times, Aunty Jane had also talked about going to Hawaii, Florida and Crete. Molly even asked her mother.

"Hmm, that *is* interesting," said Mum. "Perhaps she's ... er ... travelling around. Four weeks is quite a long time, after all. I tell you what, we'll wait until the postcards start arriving. Then we'll know where she's been."

Aunty Jane always sent lots of post-cards when she went away. She liked as many of her friends as possible to know what a good time she was having and to tell them how sorry she felt for them, stuck at home.

But this time was different. Day after day passed and not a single postcard arrived for Molly, although she waited for the postman every day.

Molly was very excited when it was finally time for Aunty Jane to come home. Apart from anything else, Aunty Jane brought exciting holiday presents. Molly already had a large pink hat, a grass skirt and some embroidered slippers from her neighbour's holidays in previous years.

"She's here! She's here!" cried Molly, when she heard a taxi pull up next door. She peered out of the window as Aunty Jane, wearing dark glasses and a scarf over her head, hurried into her home, motioning the taxi driver to follow her with her luggage.

"I'm going over to see how she got on," said Molly, thinking of the holiday

present, but her mother, who had been peering too, held her back with a rather thoughtful look.

"I think we'll just let Aunty Jane have a chance to relax after her journey," she said. "I'm quite sure she'll call on us as soon as she has rested. She'll want to crow ... I mean, she'll want to tell us all about the wonderful places she's been."

But Aunty Jane did not call round. Although Molly waited eagerly until her bedtime, there was no sign of Aunty Jane.

"Well, I'm surprised, too," said her mum, "but, you know, sometimes people pick up horrible tummy bugs and things when they're on holiday. Maybe she isn't feeling too good at the moment. I'm sure she'll be round in the morning."

As it turned out, however, it was three days before Aunty Jane appeared. She was still wearing her dark glasses and looked, somehow, strangely different. It was some time before Molly could work out why. At last, she decided it was quite a lot of little things. For a start, Aunty Jane was not wearing nearly so much jewellery. She wore

a dress with long sleeves that had buttons right up to the neck. Her nails, usually so long and red, were short and not painted at all. It made her hands look much older, somehow. Aunty Jane's hair wasn't quite so full and glossy either. The final difference took longer for Molly to spot. Then she realized what it was. Aunty Jane wasn't wearing any perfume.

Molly was puzzled, but she didn't get really suspicious until she happened to overhear her parents talking.

"Honestly, Dave, I wouldn't have known her," Molly's mum was telling her husband. "She looked like a completely different person. Well, actually, she looked quite inhuman."

"It looks like your suspicions were right, then," said Molly's dad. "It's a whole new Aunty Jane."

Molly went to bed with those words ringing in her ears. A whole new Aunty Jane... She was just drifting off to sleep when she sat up with a start. What if it wasn't Aunty Jane at all? What if it was an imposter, who had met Aunty Jane on holiday and... Molly shuddered. It was too horrible to think about.

It wasn't until the next morning that Molly had her idea about Aunty Jane being an alien. It made sense, though. An alien would get things like height and hair colour right, but it wouldn't have any idea about what Aunty Jane was really *like*. It wouldn't know, for example, that Aunty Jane just would never *ever* appear in public without having her nails done. And if she wouldn't go to bed without perfume, then she certainly wouldn't walk around without it. Molly felt brave and excited. She was determined to find out if she was right.

It's not very easy finding out if someone is an alien or not. Molly called on her neighbour the next morning and kept her eyes peeled for telltale signs.

"Did you have a nice holiday?" she asked, thinking that it was odd to wear sunglasses inside your own house on a day that wasn't even particularly sunny.

"It was gorgeous," said Aunty Jane.

"You didn't get very brown," the little girl said.

"Of course not, Molly, you know how dangerous the sun can be," said her neighbour, sounding more like her old self. "I was careful to keep in the shade as much as possible. I'm sorry I haven't got any pictures to show you, but as you know, I went away to rest. The run-of-the-mill tourist attractions are for others. I prefer to be tranquil and soak up the atmosphere of a place. Could you pass me that glass of water, please? I've got a little headache and want to take my pills. Oh, yes, what a dear girl you are. They're in my bag. Thank you."

But Molly, concentrating hard on not spilling the water, dropped the bag as she crossed the room.

"Oh, sorry!" she cried. "Don't worry, I'll pick it all up."

She set down the glass and started to shovel make-up, comb, pills, money, old receipts, train tickets and Aunty Jane's passport back into the bag. Aunty Jane, who a moment before had been lounging langorously on the sofa, suddenly leapt forward, crying, "No! No! I'll do it! You'll put everything in the wrong place!" She snatched the passport from Molly's hands ... but she was too late. Molly had looked down at the open passport and noted a very significant date.

Now mental arithmetic wasn't Molly's strongest skill, so it wasn't until she went home later that afternoon that she had a chance to sit down with a pencil and paper and do some working out. She knew when Aunty Jane was born and she knew the date today. She should, she was sure, be able to work out how old her neighbour—or whoever or whatever was pretending to be her, was today. But the sum seemed very tricky.

No matter what Molly did, she came up with a figure that couldn't possibly be right. In the end, she went through to where her mother was painting a chair in the garage and asked, casually, how old a person born on Aunty Jane's birthdate would be today.

Molly's mum didn't have to think long. "They'd be fifty-nine," she said. "Why?" She looked up at her daughter.

The look of horror on Molly's face gave the game away at once. The little girl's mother made several mental leaps, guessed right and gasped.

"Molly! You don't mean that's... How did you find out? *Well!*"

By the time Molly had finished explaining how she knew, her mother was giggling so much she couldn't carry on painting.

"I must go and tell your dad," she said. "This will really make him laugh."

At which, Molly sat down hard on the garage floor and burst into tears.

"It's not funny at all!" she sobbed. "It means she's an alien! They didn't know how old she really was, so they guessed! And they got it wrong! What have they done with the old Aunty Jane?"

It took some time for Molly's parents to decipher this line of reasoning. When they finally realized what was worrying the little girl, they exchanged a long look.

"This is ridiculous," said Molly's mum. "I'm going to go next door and have a few words with Jane. She's the best person to sort this out once and for all."

Later that evening, when Molly was tucked up in bed, Aunty Jane came and sat down beside her.

"Molly," she said, "you know that you should always tell the truth, don't you? Well, I sometimes don't quite do that. It's silly really. You see, I loved being young and pretty, like you, and I hate the idea of getting old. So I pretend to be younger than I am. I really am fifty-nine. Ugh! It sounds horrible! I don't think anyone really believes I'm thirty-eight, but it makes me feel better. And that's why I went away. I didn't go on holiday at all. I went to see a nice man who did a bit of snipping here and there to make me look younger. Only it takes a while for it to work. They don't let you have painted nails in the clinic and I can't wear perfume until my face is quite better. *Then* I'll look more gorgeous than ever, of course! But it really is me under these glasses and I'm still your Aunty Jane."

Molly snuggled down with a smile.

"Good," she said. "I don't know why you had to see the nice man, though. I still think you're the prettiest person I've ever seen."

And who can blame Aunty Jane if, passing Molly's mum wiping her painty fingers on her jeans in the doorway, she didn't look just a tiny bit triumphant?

The Bungling Burglar

Strangely enough, it wasn't Graham or his dad or his mum who first noticed that the house had been burgled. It was Alphonse. Most of the time, the Norman family thought of Alphonse as a huge but useless hound who ate them out of house and home and had no idea how to behave with decent furniture. Luckily, the Normans didn't have any decent furniture.

This time, however, Alphonse had something of a triumph. As soon as the family came down to breakfast, he began acting in a strange way—well, stranger than usual anyway. He made sure that his audience was fully assembled, trotted over to the corner of the room, sat down, lifted up his head and howled. It was a howl that might have summoned long-lost wolf ancestors from the dead. It was a howl that made Mrs. Norman cover her ears and Mr. Norman drop his coffee. It was a sound unlike anything that Alphonse had made in the past three years, since he had arrived as a puppy.

Graham hurried over to the dog and crouched down.

"What's the matter, Alf?" he asked. "Have you got a pain somewhere. Is it your teeth? Is it your tummy? A splinter in your paw? Someone trod on your tail?" (At this point, Graham looked accusingly at his father, who had been known to be careless about how he placed his feet near Alphonse's basket.)

Alphonse responded by hanging his head and looking up in a beseeching way.

"Give me a clue, Alf," pleaded his master. "Where does it hurt?"

Alphonse cast his eyes upwards, as if to say, "For goodness sake, I'm not in *pain*. I'm trying to tell you something perfectly simple and why you're too dense to spot it for yourselves, I can't imagine." Then he clambered wearily to his feet and trotted across the room to stand with his nose pointed towards the fireplace.

The eyes of the family followed the dog, and it was then that Mrs. Norman spotted what was wrong.

"My lady!" she cried. "My dancing lady! Oh no!"

Lying in the hearth was a figurine of a lady in a blue crinoline twirling around. It was an ornament that Mrs. Norman loved very much, even if her enthusiasm was not shared by the rest of the family. Now, the lady lay there—minus her arms.

"Oh dear," said Mr. Norman and tried to keep a blank look on his face.

This was too much for his wife.

"Oh, that's typical," she said. "If it was something of yours that was broken, we'd all have to go into mourning for a month. If anyone touched one of your precious CDs, there'd be a full-scale post-mortem and an investigation that Scotland Yard would be proud of. But just because it's my ornament and something you didn't care for, it's 'Oh dear'! Thank you very much!"

Mr. Norman tried to retrieve the situation by going to fetch the brush and dustpan, but his wife seized them fiercely.

"Leave her alone!" she cried in a way that betrayed the years she had spent at drama school twenty years earlier.

It was only when the family was at the breakfast table that Graham wondered out loud how the accident could possibly have happened.

"The lady was quite heavy," he said, "and high up on the mantelpiece. I don't see how she could have fallen down. A breeze or a slammed door wouldn't have done it. And it's much too high for Alf to have jumped up."

"That's right," said Mrs. Norman. "How *could* it have happened? Let's go and look."

Gazing wistfully at their cooling breakfasts, Graham and his dad got up and followed her into the next room. In silence and very dutifully, they examined the scene of the crime. They all agreed that there was no way the figurine could have fallen by accident, unless, as Mr. Norman suggested, there had been a freak earth tremor the night before.

"But none of my other ornaments have fallen down," said Mrs. Norman. "Surely a tremor wouldn't just knock over one figurine? In any case, wouldn't Alphonse have howled *then*?"

Mr. Norman embarked on a lengthy explanation of resonance and sympathetic vibrations but he was out of his depth and the other two members of his family could see that clearly.

"It's a mystery and that's all," said Mr. Norman at last. The family returned to the kitchen to find that Alphonse had eaten all the breakfasts and removed himself from the scene.

"Not much mystery here," said Mrs. Norman grimly, surveying an eggy pawprint on the tablecloth.

Next morning, Alphonse was shut in the hallway when Mrs. Norman, the last member of the family to go to bed, carefully shut all the doors and went upstairs herself. The next morning, as the first person downstairs, she gave a wail of distress that brought a sleepy Mr. Norman and a curious Graham running.

"What is it, Mum?" asked Graham. "Is Alf all right?"

"More than all right," replied Mrs. Norman drily, "I should say."

She nodded her head towards the sitting room. Alphonse was lying asleep on the sofa, which was strictly forbidden.

"What I want to know," said Mrs. Norman, looking accusingly at her son and her husband, "is how he got in there. I'm absolutely certain that I shut the sitting room door last night before I went to bed."

"Clever old Alphonse must have learned to lift the latches with his nose," said Mr. Norman.

Mrs. Norman was not impressed.

"Sometimes I wonder if you and I have been living in the same house for the last twenty years, Richard," she said. "Has it entirely escaped your attention that all our doors have knobs, not latches? I utterly fail to see how a dog could have learnt to turn the knobs. In any case, they're quite stiff. And as if that wasn't enough, the doors were *closed* when I came downstairs this morning."

"Well, Mum," ventured Graham cautiously, "are you sure you didn't shut Alphonse into the sitting room last night? It would be easy to do."

Mrs. Norman sank down on to the bottom step of the stairs and put her head in her hands in mock despair.

"Sometimes I think I'm the only one in this house with any kind of a brain," she said. "When I shut up all the doors last night, I made absolutely sure that Alphonse was out here, in the hall. He was lying in his bed under the stairs. I'd be willing to swear to it in a court of law, if necessary," she finished dramatically.

Mr. Norman and his son exchanged a look that said, "She's imagining things" and went into the kitchen, where an odd scene met their eyes.

In front of the cooker was a bowl, a spoon, a packet of cereal and a jug of milk. They were carefully positioned as if on a table—but they were on the floor.

"Does this look like something a dog could do? asked Mrs. Norman. "In any case, I fail to see how Alphonse could have been simultaneously sleeping behind a closed door in the sitting room and helping himself to breakfast behind a closed door in the kitchen."

It was a good point.

"Well," said Graham, logic leading him to an unpleasant conclusion, "if it wasn't you, Dad, and it wasn't you, Mum, and it wasn't me, then it must have been…"

"Burglars!" screamed Mrs. Norman. "Oh my goodness, we'll all be murdered in our beds!"

"No, no, my dear. The burglar, if he was here, is gone, and we're all safe," said Mr. Norman soothingly. "We must phone the police."

It was the right thing to do, but still Mr. Norman spent an embarrassing ten minutes trying to explain to a sergeant on the other end of the phone that he was ringing to complain that there was a dog on his sofa and cereal on his kitchen floor.

No, he agreed, nothing had been stolen as far as they could see. No, there was no sign of a forced entry. What was he complaining about? Well, someone had been in his

house, without permission, and in the middle of the night. Wasn't that something to complain about?

The sergeant advised Mr. Norman to be extra careful to lock all his doors and windows that night and not to hesitate to call if anything further happened. In the meantime, it sounded as though he had had a lucky escape but there was little that the police could do."

Mr. Norman, muttering about taxpayers' money, put the phone down and helped his wife to clear up the kitchen and clear out the dog. It was typical, he thought, of Alphonse to have slept through the arrival of a burglar and not made a sound. If Graham wasn't so fond of him…

The following evening, all three members of the Norman family helped to lock up the house. It was like the launching of a space mission.

"Back door locked?"

"Check!"

"Front door locked?"

"Check!"

"Windows secure?"

"Check! Check! Check!"

"Dog shut in hall?"

"Check! Woof!"

"Everyone ready to go upstairs?"

"Check! Goodnight! Goodnight! Goodnight!"

The next morning, three figures in dressing gowns gathered on the landing and synchronized their watches.

"After you," said Mr. Norman politely to his wife.

The family crept downstairs. Alphonse was still asleep under the stairs. The doors of the hallway were all firmly closed. They looked into the kitchen. Everything seemed fine. With growing confidence, Graham strode over to the sitting room door and flung it open. There in the middle of the carpet was a strange edifice. Five cushions were piled one on top of the other. Then there was a vase. On top of that, a book was precariously balanced.

"What on earth...?" Mr. Norman took a step on to the carpet. His tread was not light at the best of times. Now, it had the same result as a sudden small earth

tremor. The balanced book crashed to the floor. The vase and the cushions followed it. None of this would have mattered so much if the vase had not turned out to be full to the brim with orange juice. A sticky mess oozed out over the beige carpet.

The Norman family held a council of war in the kitchen.

"I know it's weird, but we can't call the police," said Mr. Norman, still smarting from his last encounter with the local station. I know just how the conversation will go. 'Was anything stolen?' No. 'Was any damage done?' Well, only by me. 'Were the locks forced or the windows broken?'

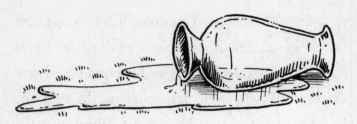

No. I cannot," Mr. Norman went on, "ask the police to come and investigate a pile of cushions. You must see that."

Sadly, Mrs. Norman did see that. But she was badly shaken.

"Do you know what I'm thinking?" she hissed. "Poltergeists! Horrible ghostly things that throw stuff around. We've got one! I can feel it!"

"It's got a very odd sense of humour," said Mr. Norman. "I never liked those cushions, you know."

"They were *beautiful*!"

Mrs. Norman felt inclined to make another theatrical gesture. Sometimes she felt it was high time she returned to the stage. Sometimes her husband and son thought so, too.

"There is only one thing we can do," said Graham, practically. "We either have a particularly bungling burglar, who seems unable to grasp the fact that he's supposed to steal something while he's in here, or we have some other kind of ... er ... manifestation. The only way we can find out is to watch and catch him in the act. We can take it in turns tonight."

It was a good plan, but Mrs. Norman declared that her nerves were in shreds and quite unequal to the task. Mr. Norman declared that once he was asleep he was dead to the world and quite impossible to

wake. Not for the first time, Graham decided that the task was his alone.

Late that night, after giving Alf full instructions about how to behave, Graham went up to bed as usual. When he heard his parents come up, he waited half an hour. Then he silently slipped out of his room and downstairs, reminding Alf to be quiet in a stage whisper his mother would have been proud of.

Under the stairs, Graham shared Alf's basket. The hours passed slowly and it was terribly tempting to go to sleep, but Graham kept reminding himself that he was upholding the honour of Alf, who was still strangely under suspicion although it was obvious that he could have had a paw in none of the odd occurrences.

At half past two, Graham heard a creaking sound. He stiffened, grasping his torch more tightly, and waited. He was

pretty sure that poltergeists didn't creak, whatever else they did.

As the creaking grew louder and louder, Graham could bear the waiting no longer. He jumped out of his hiding place and shone the torch ... straight into the blank face of his sleepwalking father. As he watched, Mr. Norman walked calmly to a pot-plant he particularly loathed and began calmly to pluck the leaves from it.

Graham rapidly considered his options. What was more likely to bring about family harmony? A suspected poltergeist or a proved ornament-smashing and pot-plant pillaging father? It was not a difficult decision. Gently, Graham led his father back to bed and went back downstairs to find the encyclopedia. He decided he needed to know a lot more about poltergeists, now that he knew they had one.

The Garden
of
Grumbles

When people passed 3, Acacia Drive, they hurried and looked with keen interest at the other side of the road. It wasn't that they wanted to avert their eyes from the truly ghastly patch of dirt and weeds that was supposed to be a front garden, although that would have been reason enough. No, it was simply that they did not want to have to talk to old Mr. Madget, who was almost certainly standing miserably in the middle of his small plot like a huge spider waiting to pounce on unwary passers-by.

What was so awful about talking to Mr. Madget? I'm sure you've met people like him. He didn't have a pleasant thing to say about anything or anybody. In the old man's world, everything was out to get him. A typical exchange might go something like this:

"Good morning, Mr. Madget!"

"What's good about it?"

"Well, the sun is shining and the birds are singing, Mr. Madget!"

"It'll be raining by lunchtime."

"Ah, well, and how are you?"

"My back's bad. My waterworks aren't what they used to be. The dog's been sick in the kitchen."

At this point, even the hardiest and most cheery neighbour usually hurried on. They really did *not* want to hear about

Mr. Madget's internal plumbing. Very occasionally, however, a brave soul would try to change the subject.

"So, are you thinking of doing some gardening then? Your plot could do with brightening up a bit."

"No point. This soil won't grow a thing. When my Margaret was alive it was a picture, but since they put the gas main down the street, it's been doomed. Not a flower. And anything that starts to grow soon gets black spots or white mould or flies or slugs and dies."

Now, any self-respecting slug or snail would want to protest at that. There was nothing in Mr. Madget's garden that any slug would deign to touch.

Why, you may ask, was Mr. Madget so horribly depressed and depressing? It had happened very gradually after the death of his wife. What the old man really wanted was sympathy and someone to take an interest in him again, but the way he moaned and groaned put everyone off.

"He isn't the only person in the world with troubles," said his neighbour Mrs. Matthews briskly. "I've offered to give him a hand with his garden more than once, but I won't force myself where I'm not wanted."

To be fair, most of us would not want Mrs. Matthews' busy-body ways in our gardens, either, but Mr. Madget had never even given her a chance.

Mr. Madget wasn't much of an oil-painting himself. As the years went by, his cardigan became holier, his trousers got shabbier, and his slippers should have been thrown away as a health hazard years ago. Mr. Madget only bothered to shave when he thought about it, which wasn't often, and even then he didn't do a very good job. Cleaning the mirror in his bathroom would have helped, but he would have said, "What's the point? It'll only get dirty again."

The years passed. Pretty soon, even weeds wouldn't grow in Mr. Madget's garden. Then, one day in spring, Mrs. Matthews unexpectedly made another effort. She arrived one morning with two lads from her husband's company and, to Mr. Madget's amazement, opened his front gate without asking and beckoned her team to come inside.

It was typical of the woman that she did not even begin to consult her neighbour about her plans. Instead, she simply told him what was going to happen.

"Barry and Gary here," she told him, "are going to neaten up your garden a bit. They're perfectly happy to do it and will be out of your way by teatime. Why don't you go inside so that you don't get in the w... I mean, why don't you go and put your feet up while we get on. It'll all look much better when we've finished."

Mr. Madget blinked.

"No," he said.

"Nonsense, dear man!" breezed Mrs. Matthews. "Who wouldn't want a nice neat garden with a few bedding plants if he could get it *with no effort and no expense*? Now, why not go and make yourself a nice cup of tea?"

"No," said Mr. Madget.

"Whatever can you mean?" laughed his neighbour. "Ha, ha, ha, ha! Don't pay any attention to him, boys. He doesn't mean it, really."

"I do," said Mr. Madget. "And what's more, if you don't get yourselves off my land immediately, I'm going to phone the police. You're trespassing. That's what you're doing!" And he went on in the same vein, using some none-too-pleasant language for a good three minutes while Mrs. Matthews stood there getting redder and redder in the face with every word he uttered.

"Why, you miserable old man!" she cried, when he paused for breath. "All I'm trying to do is help you!"

"I don't want your help," growled Mr. Madget. "Now, I'm counting to ten. One, two…"

With a cry of fury, Mrs. Matthews shooed her helpers out into the road and disappeared into her own house, banging the door behind her.

Inside her own neat home, Mrs. Matthews regrouped her forces. She put Plan B into immediate operation. Mr. Madget watched and commented as Barry and Gary erected a six-foot-high fence between his property and his neighbour's. There was nothing he could say about it, as the fence was technically on her land, but he wondered all the same why on earth she was bothering.

The answer soon came. Mrs. Matthews was moving home and she wanted to get the best possible price for her house. It was this and not kindheartedness that had prompted her to offer the services of Barry and Gary. She was very much afraid

that no one would want to live next door
to the pigsty that was number three.

But somebody did. The sale went
though remarkably quickly. Mr. Madget,
of course, was completely unaware of this,
cut off as he was by the high fence. He
didn't see a van arrive, full of pretty pieces
of furniture and pots of flowers.

The first Mr. Madget knew about
his new neighbour was when a sound of
thwacking and banging came from the
other side of the fence one morning.

"Oh dear. Oh dear," said a voice.
"This is harder than I thought."

A couple of minutes later, after a good deal more banging and thwacking, a jagged hole appeared in the fence a foot or so from the top and a cheery face peered through it.

"Oh, hello!" she said. "You must be Mr. Madget. I'm Hetty Baynes. How nice to meet you! I think it will be a lot better when this old fence is down, don't you?"

Mr. Madget was so surprised, he actually said "Hello!" back. He spoilt this first friendly impression a moment later, however, by adding, "What do you have to make so much noise for? I can hardly hear myself think."

"Oh, you're a *thinker*, Mr. Madget. How interesting," enthused Hetty Baynes. "I never had much education myself, but I do like to meet people with interesting ideas. I'm so looking forward to knowing you better. As for the noise, there's no help for it, I'm afraid. Of course, it would be over quicker if you could just give me a hand by pulling on the fence while I bash it at the bottom."

Rather to his own surprise, Mr. Madget, still glowing from the news that he had interesting thoughts, did help. The fence was soon down.

"I'll just go and make you a cup of tea to thank you," said Mrs. Baynes. "Would you like to step inside? I'm still in a bit of a mess, I'm afraid."

Mr. Madget looked down at his grubby clothes and his regrettable slippers and shook his head.

"Never mind," smiled Mrs. Baynes. "I'll bring it out here. We can have a picnic in your garden."

Five minutes later, the vicar, feeling a little guilty as he hurried past miserable Mr. Madget's front garden as usual, was astonished to see the old man and a sprightly lady taking tea and cake, perched on two deckchairs. It looked as if it was pretty good cake, too.

Mr. Madget couldn't remember the last time he had had tea and cake that tasted so good. On second thoughts, he could. The old man's eyes filled with tears as he remembered the cosy teas in front of the fire that he used to share with his much-loved Margaret.

"This is very good," he said gruffly.

Mrs. Baynes looked at her neighbour with a kindly eye. She didn't know why he was so unhappy, but she could guess. She had been through a very bad time herself when her own husband died. But she didn't like to intrude so early in their acquaintance. Instead, she looked around at the garden.

"You are lucky to have such a sunny spot," she said. "Mine is overshadowed by that acacia tree. Do you spend much time out here?"

"Yes," grunted Mr. Madget, his mouth a little over-full with cake.

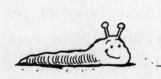

"But you don't care for gardening?"

Mr. Madget indicated the stick by his side.

"Bad leg," he said.

Mrs. Baynes laughed. "My husband Gordon used to say, 'You can lean on a spade as well as a stick,'" she said.

"It doesn't seem to make a lot of difference," said the old man. "I did try after... I did try, but everything died. No point in going on like that."

"Hmmm, I wonder why you had such bad luck," said Mrs. Baynes. She was the first person ever to think that it wasn't entirely Mr. Madget's fault.

"Well, I suppose I didn't try very hard," muttered the old man. "Might give it another go, I suppose, one day."

"I would so admire you if you did," said his neighbour. "It's not easy to go back to things that didn't work. Now, you mustn't keep me here chatting all day. I've got a whole house to sort out. I hope we'll meet again soon, Mr. Madget."

She stretched out her hand. Mr. Madget shook it. He realized suddenly that he hadn't touched another human being for four years.

"Glad to meet you, Mrs. Baynes," he said gruffly.

"Hetty, please," she laughed.

Mr. Madget shuffled and coughed. "I'm George," he said.

Next morning, Mr. Madget took a bold step. He threw out his disgusting old slippers and pulled on the boots he had not worn for years. Then he found his spade in the spare bedroom and went out into his garden. Digging, when you haven't done it for a long, long time, is hard work. As a matter of fact, it's hard work even if you've done it recently. Mr. Madget felt like giving up after about seven minutes of sustained effort.

But just as he was going to fling down his spade and dig his slippers out of the dustbin, a friendly voice came from over the fence.

"I saw you working so hard out there and I wondered if you'd like some lemonade. I made it myself. It must be very hot, working like that. You put me to shame, I must say."

Mr. Madget accepted the lemonade. It tasted like heaven. After that, he felt obliged to dig a bit more. Next time he was about to flag, a plate of ham sandwiches appeared over the fence. In the middle of the afternoon, when the old man felt he really couldn't go on any more, a cup of tea and another piece of the delicious cake arrived. Each snack was accompanied by something even better— kind words and a friendly interest. By the time that Mr. Madget staggered in at the end of the afternoon, the whole plot was dug over. It was bare, but it looked a lot better.

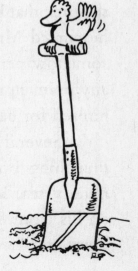

It took Mr. Madget two weeks to recover from his bout of digging. During the time that he lay flat on his back in bed, he cursed Mrs. Baynes several times for somehow persuading him that there was any point in making an effort. He cursed himself for being such a fool even more.

Several times, as he lay in bed, munching bought biscuits and slurping muddy tea, Mr. Madget heard a tapping on his front door. He was pretty sure he knew who it was. His first instinct was to hobble downstairs and let in what was almost certainly something tasty to eat. He quite liked the idea of seeing Hetty Baynes again, too. During the first few days, however, he really felt too stiff and sore to move very much. After that, when he felt a little better, he suddenly looked around at his messy, dirty rooms and saw them as his neighbour would surely see them. He couldn't, he felt, possibly invite such a nice woman into such a pigsty.

After this revelation, Mr. Madget wallowed in bed for another two days feeling sorry for himself. Then it suddenly occurred to him that there was something he could do about it.

Digging was strenuous, but it was nothing like as horrible as having to clear up the house. Mr. Madget felt in was a pointless task more than once. But very, very slowly, the improvements he was making made him feel cheerier. He dug out the instruction booklet for the washing machine, which he had used on the same programme for the past four years, regardless of what he was washing, and found that not only were there other options, but the machine would work a lot better if he put washing powder in it.

Late one night, when he was sure that no one would be about, Mr. Madget set off for the twenty-four-hour store at the end of the road and bought a few household essentials. Actually, he had to make three trips to carry them all. It had been some time since cleaning items had entered the house.

By the time he had finished, Mr. Madget needed to lie down again. The house wasn't perfect by any means, but it

looked as if someone cared for it. Mr. Madget dusted a photograph of Margaret with care and put it in the centre of the mantelpiece. She looked, he thought, as if she approved.

Next time there came a little tap on the door, he opened it, but it wasn't Mrs. Baynes who stood there. Mr. Madget felt a pang of disappointment as he recognized the vicar who usually hurried past.

"I'm sorry to disturb you, Mr. Madget," he said, "but I wondered if I could have a word with you? It's about Mrs. Baynes next door."

Mrs. Baynes, it seemed, had been taken seriously ill and rushed to hospital a few days before. She would be there for some time, but, as she knew no one in the area, she had few visitors and was feeling very low.

"The only person she seems to want to see," said the vicar, sounding as if he hardly believed it himself, "is you, Mr. Madget. She keeps worrying about you, as she hasn't seen you around for a while."

The vicar had scarcely left the house when Mr. Madget, changed into a clean shirt and tie and wearing a jacket, set off to catch the bus to the hospital. It was a route he knew well, for he had visited every day in the last weeks of his wife's life. He had sworn never to set foot in the place again, but now that hardly seemed to matter. On the way through the foyer, he suddenly had a thought and stopped to buy some flowers.

He hardly recognized Hetty when he saw her. All the life seemed to have left her, and she could hardly raise a smile when he sat down. Mr. Madget recognized the signs only too well. He pushed the flowers towards her.

"This won't do, you know," he said gruffly. "You've got to keep cheerful. I'm not so good at that myself, but I thought you were an expert."

Mrs. Baynes smiled weakly.

"I was," she said, "but you can only take so much…"

"Take these flowers for a start," said Mr. Madget, and Mrs. Baynes laughed.

"I was wondering if you'd like me to look after your garden while you're in here," said Mr. Madget, "while I'm doing mine. It will be no trouble. But I need you back soon to give me advice about what to plant, you know."

So that is how Mr. Madget's garden of grumbles became the jewel that passers-by now make a point of crossing the road to see. The new Mrs. Madget is proud of it, too.

And, in case you think that this is just *too* happy an ending, you might like to know that every slug and snail for miles around makes a beeline for the couple's begonias.